365 REASONS TO BE CHEERFUL

RICHARD HAPPER

365

REASONS

TO BE

CHEERFUL

MAGICAL MOMENTS TO
CHEER UP MISERABLE SODS
ONE DAY AT A TIME

PORTICO

I've chosen the stories in this book because they make me cheerful.
Can you think of any others? Send them to me: 365@richardhapper.com

First published in the United Kingdom in 2010 by
Portico Books
10 Southcombe Street
London
W14 0RA

An imprint of Anova Books Company Ltd

Illustrations by Damien Weighill (www.damienweighill.com)

ISBN 978-1-906032-96-8

A CIP catalogue record for this book is available from the British Library.

10 9 8 7 6 5 4 3 2 1

Printed in Great Britain by TJ International Ltd, Padstow, Cornwall

This book can be ordered direct from the publisher at www.anovabooks.com

While there is a chance of the world getting through its troubles, I hold that a reasonable man has to behave as though he were sure of it. If at the end your cheerfulness is not justified, at any rate you will have been cheerful.

H. G. Wells

INTRODUCTION

Every day of the year newspapers publish stories of misery, suffering, depression and general all-round grumpiness. Not because they enjoy it, but because there seems to be a lot of it going around at the moment.

But that doesn't mean we should have to wallow in it.

I am a cheerful man. I like to hear cheerful things. Not just stuff about dogs barking 'sausages' or squirrels learning to waterski, you understand. I mean the big stories that lift the heart, engage the brain and maybe even make the spirit soar a little more than it was doing when I crawled out of bed this morning.

In short, I can't stand miserable buggers.

So I started collecting a few of my favourite pick-me-up stories. Things that made me chuckle; tales that made me smile. The more I found, the more I realised how joyful this world of ours can be and how much there is to celebrate on a day-to-day basis. There are thousands of joyful stories to be told *every single day*.

From flying cows to wrestling camels, from wellies to bikinis and women's rights to martinis, from pearls to penis festivals and Las Vegas to Bacchanalia, from cheese rolling to corn circles, and dishwashers to disco dancing via diamonds the size of planets, there is a lot to be happy about. You just don't know it yet.

Of course, we all have to pay attention to the less fun stuff too, like paying the bills and getting out of bed. As I tell my cat, 'Life isn't all jelly, puss. Sometimes life is chunks, too'. There's a time and a place for being grumpy and serious.

But it's not here and it's not now. This book is about taking a happy moment to smile to yourself, about enjoying life for its own sake (and yours) and travelling to an oasis of amusement in the arid desert of the everyday. I thought it would be fun to have such a place to visit on those dull, grey and bleak Monday mornings.

Perhaps you feel the same?

If you do, join me. Take my hand and let me guide you on a year-long voyage of looking on the bright side of life every day of the year, one day at a time.

I guarantee it'll cheer you up.

Richard Happer
29th June 2010

JANUARY

THE INTERNET IS BORN

Click here to start the fun. Today in 1983, the Internet – in all its anarchic and indecent splendour – was born.

But it wasn't like someone just pressed a button and whoosh! up went the muck. Computer networks had been around for years – governments, universities and the military all had machines that could 'talk' to each other. The big problem was that those separate networks couldn't understand one another properly. To one computer, some data might represent operational codes for twin Russian missile silos, while another was decoding it as a picture of Pamela Anderson with her top off. Clearly something had to be done.

So it was on this day that the controllers of these networks started using the Internet Protocol Suite. This is a standardised format – much like how different trains run on the same line of track – that meant the networks now had a universal structure for data to travel along. This set the scene for the creation of the World Wide Web (see 12 November) – a super-snazzy train that runs on those tracks, and makes sharing information via billions of pages of websites even more easy and enjoyable.

NEW YEAR'S DAY
(FOR PROCRASTINATORS)

Another New Year, another new leaf not turned over? Cheer up – history is full of famous artists and inventors who achieved amazing things despite being bloody lazy.

Leonardo da Vinci started painting a friend's wife, but didn't get around to finishing it for *sixteen years* – it turned out to be the *Mona Lisa*. Albert Einstein dithered for so long deciding it was 'mc²' that 'E' equalled, that he practically went back in time. While Douglas Adams, author of *The Hitchhiker's Guide to the Galaxy*, once said, 'I love deadlines. I like the whooshing sound they make as they fly by'.

So it's okay, you don't have to get absolutely everything done today. The New Year's resolutions can wait, particularly when there's always the greatest labour-saving device of today at your disposal – tomorrow.

RAISE YOUR GLASS ... TO THE
DRINKING STRAW!

Though kids in 1888 had Coca-Cola, Dr Pepper and Schweppes fizzy drinks to slurp on, no one had yet made a proper drinking straw – until Marvin Stone saved the day – on this very day.

People had tried making drinking straws out of

hollow grass, but they went soggy and made your pop taste like hay. Rubbish. Then Marvin had his brainwave. He wrapped a piece of paper around a pencil and coated it in wax, thus stiffening the paper and waterproofing it too. Soon kids all over America were bubbling sarsaparilla. The drinking straw was a hit.

More importantly, desperate people the world over *finally* had something to clutch at.

EX-WRESTLER SWORN IN ...

Life would be a lot brighter, and more cheerful, if more politicians were like Jesse Ventura. Most people running for office keep their wilder opinions to themselves and try to paper over their speckled pasts, but Ventura is refreshingly different.

He admitted that in the early 1970s he was a full-patch member of an outlaw motorcycle gang and organised crime syndicate, The Mongols. Ventura supports the legalisation of prostitution, to protect the health of the workers in an industry that he believes will always exist. He also acted in the 1987 movie *Predator* with the future Governor of California, Arnold Schwarzenegger. When he was elected Governor of Minnesota, his supporters adopted the slogan 'My governor can beat up your governor'.

Only in America . . .

TWELFTH NIGHT

Today's cheer comes from the very ancient festival of mischief, merrymaking and general mucking about – Twelfth Night. For one day, life's natural order was reversed, so masters attended servants, and servants ordered masters around (although presumably not too harshly if they still wanted to have jobs the next day!). A peasant was proclaimed The Lord of Misrule, and it was his job to keep the chaos alive the whole day. This was acheived by pumping everyone full of wassail – a medieval type of alcopop.

MOTHER TERESA HEALS THE WORLD

Mother Teresa brought a special kind of cheer into the world. For forty-five years, her kindly face and gentle spirit (not to mention her funny headscarf thing) were instantly recognisable as a symbol of hope and faith to the people most desperately in need of it – and the people of Calcutta will never forget this very special day. Today in 1929 she came to save their souls with her Missionaries of Charity that is still working miracles now. God bless.

GET YOUR SKATES ON

For centuries, people had enjoyed the winter pastime of skating on frozen lakes. It warmed your cockles and a put smile on your face (as it still does now), but there was always the common risk of falling through the ice into fatally cold water. Then a clever fellow called John Gamgee opened his Glaciarium today in London in 1876.

Gamgee knew that you could create a compound that would lower temperatures. So he mixed layers of earth, cow hair and timber, over which he ran copper pipes carrying a solution of glycerine, ether, nitrogen peroxide and water. This cooled the pipes. All Gamgee had to do then was put water on top and *voilà* – the world's first artificial ice rink.

Y.M.C.A.
'MACHO TYPES WANTED: MUST DANCE AND HAVE A MOUSTACHE'

So ran the 1977 advert placed by music producer Jacques Morali seeking a new 'concept' band. Morali wanted to capitalise on the vibrant gay disco scene centred around New York's Greenwich Village (hence the band's name).

'Y.M.C.A.' was a global hit and is still commonly regarded as one of the best pop records of all time. And you'd have to have a heart of stone not to smile, sing, or dance along, any (and every) time you heard it.

Well, today in 1978, the song was released on an unsuspecting public for the first time . . . and, boy, the charts were never the same again.

For the record, only the cowboy, the brave and the sailor were actually gay.

THE FIRST MODERN CIRCUS OPENS

By the eighteenth century, acrobats and performing animals had been cheering up adults and terrifying infants for many generations. But the acts always performed solo, not as elements in a grander show. Enter Philip Astley, a brilliant – maybe even the greatest – showman.

In 1768, Astley set up a horse-riding show in a field behind what is now Waterloo station in London and his phenomenal horseback acrobatics soon wowed the big crowds. Uniquely, it was Astley who had his horses run in a circle. This put the action of the show right in the middle of the crowd while also generating centrifugal force to give the rider added stability. His ring diameter of forty two feet is still the standard used in every circus today.

And, should you be coulrophobic, it is Astley you have to blame for introducing clowns in between the main events, therefore bolstering their ability to terrorise for several centuries to come.

RUBBER-DUCK INDEPENDENCE DAY

Today in 1992, a cargo ship was battling the fury of a Pacific storm when a fearsome wave swept several of its containers clean off the deck and into the raging sea. Bad news for the companies who lost their products but great news for the 29,000 Friendly Floatees rubber-duck bath toys inside one of the sea-swept containers.

For them, this was freedom!

These yellow rubber ducks now had the whole seven seas to play in – they were determined to make the most of it. Two-thirds promptly set off south towards warmer climes, landing three

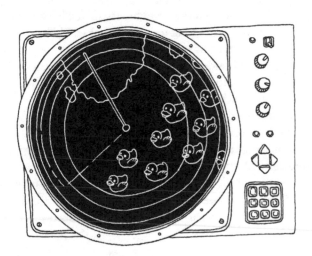

months later on the shores of Indonesia, Australia, and South America. The remaining 10,000 plastic travellers bravely bobbed north to Alaska.

There are thousands of these ducks still at sea, so if you are ever by the coast, watch out for flotsam with the magic words 'The First Years' printed on it. That duck has come a long, long way to be with you. He deserves a good home.

INSULIN IS HERE!

In 1922, a diagnosis of diabetes was a death sentence. The only variable was when the end would come – often within weeks or days. Canadian surgeon Frederick Banting, and his assistant Charles Best, had spent years trying to isolate what would later become known as insulin from the pancreas of animals. Eventually they obtained enough extract to try it out, and today, 11 January, 1922, they injected Leonard Thompson, a fourteen year-old diabetic who lay dying at the Toronto General Hospital with the first ever dose of insulin. Leonard recovered, with no obvious side-effects.

Late one night, armed with syringes of pure insulin, the doctors entered a ward of children dying from diabetes. They stopped at every bed, injecting each child as the sorrowful parents watched. They had not reached the last child when the first few began to wake from their comas to the astonished joy of their families.

DR JAMES BEDFORD

Science fiction became science fact on this day in 1967 when Dr James Bedford, a seveny-three-year-old psychology professor, became the first person to be cryonically frozen after his death. Assuming his brain hasn't turned into a slush puppy, and an advanced society actually can wake him up, he's going to be the world's first time traveller.

But although it's a (very) cool way to end your life, you have to think what it would actually be like to wake up. Would it be worth it? All your friends and family are dead, you've got antifreeze for blood and you *still* have the illness that killed you – but hey, look, an HDTV!

START-A-HOBBY DAY

Today is officially the start of Hobby Month, and a great day to pursue a new pastime.

What exactly is a hobby? Well, it might be defined as building, learning or collecting something that keeps you amused, but isn't useful. So rather than building furniture, learning Italian or collecting hard currency, you might build a scale model of Tower Bridge out of chewing gum found on Tower Bridge, learn Esperanto or collect plumbers' business cards. As always, there's a fine line between being a keen hobbyist and being a complete mentalist.

TURN ON, TUNE IN, DROP OUT

The peace movement, women's liberation, flower power and the cultural explosion of the 1960s – none of them would have happened without the Human Be-In, a 'happening' which took place in San Francisco's Golden Gate Park on this day in 1967.

The day started out as a reaction to the recent banning of LSD, and more than 20,000 people grooved to Timothy Leary's request to 'Turn on, tune in, drop out'. The event brought the ideas of the counterculture movement to the mainstream, and became a springboard for a burst of creative energy and social expression that changed popular culture forever.

It also helped popularise the concept of free love, which made the thousands of unwashed hippies who wouldn't otherwise have got laid very cheerful indeed.

AN UPLIFTING PLANE CRASH

Chesley 'Sully' Sullenberger, the captain of US Airways Flight 1549, made 155 people very cheerful on this day in 2009 when he landed his plane . . . on the Hudson River.

The plane was still ascending from take-off when a flock of suicidal Canada geese nose-dived into both engines. Sully called a nearby airfield for an emergency landing, but with zero thrust available it was clear that they weren't going to make it. So he aimed for the icy Hudson River and told passengers and crew to brace themselves. While plummeting towards the water at 150 miles per hour, he actually had the presence of mind to aim for piers with boats. The plane smashed belly first onto the water, skidded for a few blocks and came to rest just opposite the 50th Street ferry.

The captain calmly walked the complete length of the cabin – not once, but twice – to make sure that everyone else was safe before he stepped out onto the wing himself, the last man to leave the rapidly sinking airliner.

INTERNATIONAL FETISH DAY

Think you're weird for having a fetish? You're not, and today is the day to celebrate the fact that you're in great company.

In the past this sort of thing was generally kept in the closet. Particularly by people who have a fetish for closets. But now, thanks to the hard, hard work done by the BDSM community, International Fetish Day helps boost the understanding of fetishism. Celebrities have also been doing their bit: Quentin Tarantino's movies often focus on feet (podophilia, the most common fetish), Ricky Martin supposedly enjoys watersports (urolagnia), while Angelina Jolie allegedly has a soft spot for S&M (sado-masochism).

So today really is the day to get your freak on . . .

HOME VIDEO TAPING LEGAL

Next time you record an episode of your favourite TV show, you should be thankful for a landmark legal decision made on this day in 1984.

In the late 1970s, movie studios saw rising video cassette recording (VCR) sales as a threat, so Universal Studios took VCR makers Sony to court. The judges had a long think, before eventually deciding (but only by a five to four margin) that home recording was indeed fair use. They argued that by recording a show you are basically just shifting it in time. And just because a machine *could* copy something illegally, it didn't mean that Sony was responsible for each individual's actions.

Remember that the next time you Sky+ something . . .

COOK DISCOVERS HAWAII ... PHEW!

Stunning scenery, spectacular surf, a tropical climate, welcoming locals, *Magnum PI* . . . Hawaii certainly has a lot to make you cheerful.

Captain Cook and his crew also had the good fortune to drop anchor in Kealakekua Bay, the sacred harbour of the local fertility god, just as the natives were starting their worship today in 1778. The Englishmen, with their strange ships and attire, had clearly been sent from the heavens, and for the next month the visitors made the most of their luck. The people were particularly fascinated by the Europeans' use of iron, and Cook bought provisions with the metal.

His crew, on the other hand, swapped iron nails for sex with the Hawaiian females. Well you would, wouldn't you?

MIAMI CHILLS

Florida, *the* Sunshine State, had snowfall for the first and only time today in 1977. Not so cheerful for those sun-bleached Floridians, you might think, but very satisfying for us grey-skinned Brits.

Mind you, it was reported that this freak weather made for a great day. Despite it being the only time that snow has fallen in the city, *ever*, the transport network did not shudder to a halt and the newspapers did not implode in hysterics. Everyone just got on with things and had a bit of a laugh throwing snowballs. And with the single-day 'blizzard' lasting about as long as the average British summer, maybe we shouldn't get too cocky.

FIRST ROLL OF A COASTER

The first roller coaster was nothing more than an out-of-control mining wagon. In Pennsyvania, people enjoyed freewheeling downhill on this gravity-powered train, and it didn't take long before savvy mine owners were soon charging fifty cents a time to coast with the coal.

A chap called LaMarcus Adna Thompson (born, cheerily, in a place called Licking County) saw the potential of this ride and on this day in 1885 he patented the roller coaster. It was only 600 feet long, and travelled at six miles an hour, but as fairgrounds grew, so too did the roller coasters. The reigning whopper coaster is Kingda Ka in New Jersey. The train can top 128 miles per hour and its main tower is a vomit-propelling 456 feet high.

FLIGHT OF THE CONCORDE

With its sleek design, superior service and supersonic speed, Concorde was indisputably the coolest aircraft in the skies and today in 1976 was the first day it ever flew through them.

From the outset it was an awesomely ambitious project: French and British aerospace companies agreed to work together on a supersonic airliner, but rather than be happy with Mach 1, they went straight to Mach 2.02. Nice.

In 1996, Concorde posted the fastest-ever transatlantic flight time, nipping from Heathrow to JFK in a seriously swift two hours, fifty two minutes and fifty nine seconds. That's twenty two miles a minute.

NOT THE MOST DEPRESSING DAY OF THE YEAR

A 'scientist' once calculated that the third Monday in January is the most depressing day of the year. He weighed up factors such as failed New Year diets, bleak weather and lack of money before pay-day and thus created 'Blue Monday'. Of course, this only made everyone feel worse. Until that is, when it fell on this day in 2007.

Tired of being told they ought to be depressed, people reacted against 'Blue Monday' and tried to promote cheerfulness instead. A comedy club in London launched a night called 'Gloom Aid'. There is also a 'Beat Blue Monday' campaign (beatbluemonday.org.uk) and today people are encouraged to fight the seasonal blues and promote fun and good times instead.

CAMELS GET THE HUMP

With its ludicrous costumes and macho posturing, wrestling is always guaranteed to raise a cheer. so imagine the fun to be had then the rival combatatents are a pair of . . . camels.

For generations, people have flocked to the world championships of this proud sport, held today in the ancient town of Selçuk, Turkey. Two particularly haughty bull camels are led into a packed stadium, fetchingly saddled in the camel equivalent of spandex leotards. A female in heat is led in to get the boys revved up – she shakes her humps, bats all three pairs of eyelashes and the lads go crazy. Only they're not great fighters, camels, and after a bit of harmless snorting and leaning on each other, one decides he has lost and hoofs it towards the crowd. Cue the highlight of the day: the scrabbling out of the way as a ton of humiliated dromedary barrels towards you.

BEER IN A CAN

This amazing idea was first proposed in America in 1909, but early prototype cans either burst in transit or made the beer taste like mercury, and then a pesky thing called Prohibition got in the way. So it wasn't until this glorious day in 1935 that Krueger's Finest Beer went on sale in cans in Richmond, Virginia.

And although twenty six years is a hell of a time to wait for a beer, British drinkers had to suffer even longer – the major brewers didn't exactly have a can-do outlook to this genius new technology. Indeed, Mr Watney, of Watney Combe Reid remarked: 'I am not convinced that there would be any demand in this country for beer in cans'.

You can't help but smile at how wrong he was. Bottoms up!

UP HELLY AA

If you're looking for a night out to lift your spirits, Lerwick in Shetland is the place to be today. It hosts the festival of Up Helly Aa, which is ostensibly held to celebrate the end of the old Yule season, although history, like many attendees' heads, is a little fuzzy on the details.

It's Europe's largest fire festival with over 1,000 flaming torches brightening the night in the tiny island town. There's a thundering spirit of Norse hell-raising as squads of Viking 'guizers' roam from hall to hall, performing songs and comic sketches and imbibing the odd cup of warm mead.

AUSTRALIA DAY

Australia has so much that's worth cheering about: beautiful beaches, cosmopolitan cities, superb cultural and sporting achievements, and of course, *Neighbours*.

Today's celebrations actually commemorate the hoisting of the Union flag at Sydney Cove in 1788, proclaiming British sovereignty over the eastern seaboard of Australia. The choice of day is not without its controversies, with many Australians of indigenous heritage referring to it as 'Invasion Day'. You can see their point.

Still, it's undeniably the biggest day of the year down-under with millions of people turning out to parade, picnic and party together. So stick on something green and gold, grab some Berkshire-brewed Fosters and raise an antipodean cheer!

AMADEUS! AMADEUS!

Mozart's music, for some, can take the mind to incredible depths of emotion. But today on his birthday, we're commemorating the cheeky, filthy and fun-loving side of his music.

The 1984 film *Amadeus* famously showed the young composer's frivolity, to the annoyance of many conservative music critics. But they have only to refer to his work catalogued K.233/382d and called 'Leck mir den Arsch fein recht schön sauber' to see that the film was spot on. A canon for three voices in B-flat major, this piece was one of a set of six similar works that he wrote in Vienna in 1782. Here are its translated lyrics:

> *Lick my arse nicely,*
> *lick it nice and clean,*
> *nice and clean, lick my arse.*
> *That's a greasy desire,*
> *nicely buttered . . .*

And it goes on. While it's unsettling to think that one of the world's greatest composers was a bit of weirdo, a weirdo he was. And that cheers me up.

LEGO

Today in 1958 the patenting of Lego's world-famous bricks started a new craze still enjoyed by children of the world over – at least until they discover *Call of Duty*.

Lego is a mini-marvel of colourful toy technology – the bricks made today are still compatible with ones produced in 1958. So if you suddenly find yourself with loads of time on your hands, you can always go back and finish that giant robot you got bored with building when you were six.

THE FIRST PETROL-POWERED CAR

This should get all you petrolheads revved up – today we celebrate Karl Benz, creator of the first car in 1886.

Mind you, it's lucky he invented the thing at all. Benz's early models had steering problems, causing him to have the world's first car crash. He also had bother with his wife, Bertha. No sooner had he created the car than she borrowed it without telling him and went to visit her mother. But like all quick-thinking wives throughout the ages, she managed to deflect his wrath, pointing out that her sixty-five-mile trip was excellent publicity for the new vehicle.

She was right, and her drive from Mannheim to Pforzheim is now a popular tourist trail – the Bertha Benz Memorial Route.

ICE TO SEE YOU ...

When the average daily temperature is -10°C you need something special to keep your good cheer. That's why when the temperature drops in Quebec the whole city goes snow crazy – culminating in the Quebec Winter Carnival.

The leader of this midwinter merrymaking is 'Bonhomme' – a demented snowman with a red cap and sash. For seveteen days this mascot leads the largest snow festival in the world. Among other festivities, you can try your (gloved) hand at making snow sculptures, race a dogsled on the frozen river and, if you're truly bonkers, take a snow bath. Turn up, coat on, chill out.

POOHSTICKS

Laziness leaves you feeling guilty and dissatisfied. Idling, on the other hand, cheers the spirit wonderfully. And there can be few better ways of pleasantly idling away an afternoon than by playing Poohsticks, which for twenty five years has had its World Championships today at Day's Lock on the River Thames.

The rules of Poohsticks are simple. Find a bridge over a river, a friend and a stick each. The two of you drop your sticks in at the upstream side of the bridge and then scurry over to the other side. The first stick to appear decides the winner. Then simply repeat until sundown (or you're called in for tea, whichever is sooner).

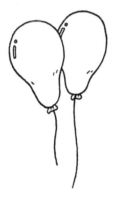

FEBRUARY

SPRING LAMBS

 It's the first day of February, and today the busiest part of lambing season gets under way. It may well be mayhem for farmers but who cares – to wayside wanderers the sight of those cute little creatures gambolling in fields brings a cheer to the heart and a rumble to the belly.

But what would put an even bigger smile on everyone's face would be to see these lovely little lambs *gambling* in a field, crouched over a miniature roulette table perhaps or playing Blackjack with cards in their little hooves, and glasses of whisky and soda by their sides.

That would really make the day, wouldn't it?

GROUNDHOG DAY

Groundhog Day isn't just a great film, it's also a real US and Canadian holiday, and a cheerful one too, as it epitomises the quirky little things in life that are worth celebrating.

This 'ancient' Pennsylvanian tradition states that if a groundhog (a kind of marmot) emerges from its burrow and doesn't see its own shadow, it will leave its winter home and winter will soon end. However, if the groundhog *does* see its shadow, he'll duck back inside and winter will continue for six more weeks. Apparently.

But regardless of what the groundhog predicts, Punxsutawney locals still party like spring is here already, with lashings of fine food and drink, speeches and music. After all, what does an overgrown squirrel *really* know about weather forecasting?

CHINESE NEW YEAR (2011)

Most major cities have a population of Chinese descent, and you can bet your boiled dumplings that they'll be partying today.

Chinese New Year falls on the second new moon after the winter solstice, so it moves around in the Gregorian calendar. The traditions of the day vary too, but there are some common customs. First, clean your home from top to bottom. This might be a chore, but it sweeps away ill fortune and clears the way for good luck to enter. Then you can deck the house with coloured-paper lanterns and other decorations and, then finally, enjoy a family feast. In the evening, the old year goes out with the bangs of thousands of firecrackers.

2011 is the Year of the Rabbit. Those born this year will be graceful, polite and cautious, with lovely big ears.

TEFLON AND ON

 If you're a fry-up fan, then today you have a Full English plate of reasons to be cheerful. Thanks to the accidental invention of Teflon (known by boffins everywhere as polytetrafluoroethylene, PTFE) by Roy Plunkett in 1938 – with his patent granted today in 1941 – you now no longer have to waste your precious time chiselling scorched eggs off your pans.

But how do they get the non-stick surface to stick to the pan? Elementary my dear reader: layers. First, the pan is blasted with grit to roughen the surface. Then a layer of PTFE is 'stickified' with some lumpy extra molecules. This makes it tacky enough to stick to the tiny craters made by the grit blasting. In fact, PTFE is so frictionless it's the only known surface that geckos can't stick to. Useful if you're planning on frying one for breakfast.

HOT WATER BOTTLE

Climbing into a pre-heated bed on a frosty night is one of those things that warms the soul as well as the body. So today in 1903 we should remember, with a cuddle of appreciation, Mr Eduard Penkala from Croatia, who patented the modern rubber hot water bottle.

For centuries people had warmed the sheets with a kind of long-handled frying pan with a lid, which you filled with the embers of the evening fire. Pretty risky, and smelly too. So hot water soon replaced burning coal and the bedwarmer became a sealed metal flask. But these were so scorchingly hot that they had to be swaddled in cloth. Penkala's stroke of genius was to combine the ideal shape with the ideal material – thick rubber. Toasty!

CARNIVAL OF VENICE

If fabulous masked balls held amid amazing architecture are the kind of thing that cheers your heart, then Venice is the place to be today. Since 1268 the world's most romantic city has been hosting what has to be one of the most glamorous festivals in the world.

For ten days every year, music floods the canals and cobbled streets of this fabulous city as equally fabulous partygoers don traditional masks to get up to as much as they can get away with. I've always thought that partying is best done incognito.

Plus, if you keep your mask on the morning after your debauchery, no one will be able to see the bags under your eyes.

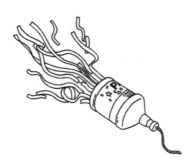

LADIES AND GENTLEMEN, WE ARE FLOATING IN SPACE

Some human achievements are just so damned cool that you can't help become giddy. And today in 1984, astronauts Bruce McCandless II and Robert L. Stewart fulfilled the dreams of a billion schoolkids when they left the cargo bay of the space shuttle Challenger and made the first untethered space walk.

The astronauts had what NASA called a 'Manned Maneuvering Unit' (MMU), although this was clearly just a La-Z-Boy chair painted white and fitted with retrorockets. Which was even cooler.

Undaunted by the possibility that a thruster might misfire and send him spinning off towards Neptune for the remainder of his career, McCandless bravely ventured 320ft out from the spacecraft and became the first human Earth-orbiting satellite.

QUEEN LIZ 2

Even if you aren't much of a royalist, you can't deny that as queens go, Elizabeth II has been one of the most popular and hardest working in British history.

Her reign started today in 1952, and at fifty eight years (and counting) is the third-longest of a British monarch – longer than those of her four immediate predecessors combined. More than 20 million of us watched her coronation on telly, with twelve million more tuning in on the radio. When she made her first visit to Australia, three-quarters of the country's *entire* population turned out to see her famous wave.

THE BEATLES ON THE ED SULLIVAN SHOW

It was ten minutes that changed the face of music forever – The Beatles stepped onto the stage of Ed Sullivan's TV entertainment showcase and blew America away. It was today in 1964.

'I Want to Hold Your Hand' had just hit No.1 and experienced newsmen were staggered by the sheer excitement of crowds wherever the band went. Big things were expected from their appearance on the show. They didn't disappoint. A record-breaking seventy-three million US viewers watched as the Fab Four performed a handful of top tunes. Pop music, television or culture would never be the same again.

'THE GREATEST PARTY IN HISTORY'

Next time you're enjoying yourself at a fundraising dinner (if that's your thing) lift a glass to Mrs Cornelia Bradley-Martin, a New York socialite who popularised the idea that having a great time could also be helpful to those who have less.

Back in 1897, New York was in a depression. Mrs Bradley-Martin believed that if the wealthy splashed some cash enjoying themselves, then thousands of working people could earn money instead of having to accept charity. And since the bigger the party, the better off everyone would be, she decided to host the most expensive costume ball in history.

Although its excesses drew a lot of criticism at the time (it cost more than $400,000 – $10 million today), the party set the template for the modern charity ball.

START FLIRTING

Today is the first day of International Flirting Week. Should you be a bachelor, remember to mark it down quickly in your 'hectic' social calendar.

Celebrated the world over, today was started to extend the romantic fun leading to Valentine's Day, and give those people who don't already have that special someone a little extra time to get their hands on one so that they don't spend the day utterly sad, pathetic and alone.

And even if you are completely rubbish at talking to the opposite sex (and who isn't?) today's celebrations should give you the confidence to speak to the object of your affection without making a total fool of yourself.

DARWIN DAY

As the birthday of one of the greatest scientists of all time, Charles Darwin, today marks a global celebration of thought and reason. It's also the perfect time to mark the total lack of thought and reason shown by winners of the 'Darwin Awards'.

These awards recognise people who, through an act of terminal stupidity, accidentally select themselves out of the gene pool and generally make things better for humanity. Like the twenty people who organised a beachfront 'Hurricane Party' – and perished when a 24-foot wave obliterated their apartment. Or the man who shot himself in the head when, instead of picking up the ringing telephone on his bedside table, he 'answered' the loaded revolver which he also kept there.

LARGEST DIAMOND IN THE GALAXY

A sky of shining stars has an almost primeval power to thrill the heart. And out in the constellation Centaurus, astronomers today in 2004 discovered the biggest reason to be cheerful.

BPM 37093 is a white dwarf star, fifty light years from Earth. It is dying: its nuclear fuel all burnt, it has collapsed in on itself to an incredible density. Once the size of our Sun, it is now the size of Earth. Its inner core is mostly carbon, with some oxygen. And just as on Earth, carbon under huge pressure forms a diamond. The diamond inside BPM 37093 is more than 4,000 kilometres across (more than one-third the diameter of Earth) and weighs ten billion trillion trillion carats. And it's just floating there in space!

6.0 6.0 6.0 6.0 6.0 6.0 6.0 6.0 6.0

For every Argentinean who marvels at Maradona's solo goal in the 1986 World Cup quarter-final, there is an Englishman who can't bear to watch it. But some sporting moments are so transcendental that even the other competitors rise to applause. The ice dancing finals at the 1984 Winter Olympics were just such an occasion.

Torvill and Dean were astonishingly good, but 'Boléro' was amazing even by their standard. It notched up nine perfect 6.0 scores, including flawless artistic impression scores from every judge. Around the rink, fans and athletes rose in triumphant awe.

Watch it online today – I guarantee it'll make you smile too.

BIRTHDAY OF PHILOSOPHER EPICURUS

Philosophy might be thought-provoking, but it doesn't normally fill you with glee – unless you follow the wisdom of Epicurus who was born today in 341 BC.

Epicurus proposed that philosophy should make people happy, mainly by freeing them from the fears implanted in them by religion. Good friends and good living paved the way to a tranquil life, and Epicurus dedicated himself to living in the moment rather than worrying about the hereafter – a revolutionary teaching that has travelled down through time.

TUTANKHAMUN'S TOMB

When Howard Carter knocked a hole through the dusty door in the Valley of the Kings today in 1923 he didn't just reveal a tomb full of gold, he opened the way to a whole new genre of danger, fun and thrill-seeking.

Carter had spent many years searching the sands of Egypt without finding the spectacular tombs that his patron Lord Carnarvon so desired. Then, under a pile of rubble, Carter uncovered the world's greatest treasure hoard.

Tutankhamun's entire coffin was made of pure gold. He was surrounded by the items essential to his royal position in the afterlife: chariots, statues and a throne all of gold; a fleet of miniature ships to help him sail to the netherworld; precious jewellery and exotic scent.

RANDOM-ACTS-OF-KINDNESS DAY

Mark Twain said, 'the best way to cheer yourself up is to try to cheer somebody else up'. And that's the basic philosophy of today: do something nice for someone else. It's great for them, and being kind is good for your health, too. Apparently, performing a generous act releases endorphins, the body's natural painkillers, giving you a 'helper's high'. This rush of euphoria is usually followed by a longer period of calm and improved emotional well-being.

So why not give it a try?

You could help someone pack their shopping, pay for their cappuccino, carry their bags to their car, oil their bike chain. Just don't do it all for the same person – such as your wife – or they'll probably get suspicious.

FIRST FLIGHT BY A ... COW

Sometimes, behind the apparently worthy façade of a news story, it's plain that someone was just having a laugh.

Take the tale of Nellie Jay. On this day in 1930, she became the first cow to fly in an aeroplane, soaring seventy two miles from Bismarck, Missouri, to St. Louis. The official purpose of this flight was 'scientific research'. The real reason however, is obvious: somebody, somewhere, was clearly very drunk.

Consider this – not content with getting the poor cow actually into the aircraft, the crew also milked her during the flight. The Guernsey produced a cool six gallons of milk that was put into paper cartons and parachuted to spectators below. No sober person could have come up with that idea.

PHONOGRAPH PATENTED

 In our day of digital music downloads, it's easy to forget that until the late 1980s the record player was the main way of listening to music and had been since Edison patented it on this day in 1878.

He had already wowed the *Dragons' Den* of the time: the editors of *Scientific American*. Edison marched into their office and set his machine on the table without even an introduction. He then turned the crank and to the amazement of the beards behind the table, the machine said, 'Good morning. How do you do? How do you like the phonograph?'

The public was equally impressed and by the turn of the century, thousands of homes were alive with the sound of pre-recorded music.

THE LOYAL VIGIL OF GREYFRIARS' BOBBY

Bobby was a Skye terrier who belonged to John Gray, a night watchman in nineteenth century Edinburgh. Dog and master were inseparable until tuberculosis took John from his companion's side in February 1858.

Gray was buried in Greyfriars Kirkyard, and once the earth was packed on the coffin and the few mourners had departed, something incredible happened. Bobby trotted across the wet grass, laid down and took up his post on his master's grave. He would remain on that single spot for the rest of his life. Bobby kept up his vigil, until he too passed away, fourteen long years later.

To this day, tourists travel thousands of miles to pay their respects to the most loyal of pooches – proof that man and dog can indeed be the best of friends.

FIRST FLYING CAR TAKES OFF

The flying car, like jet packs and hover boards, is something that really ought to be more readily available – just ask any small boy. And today in 1937, an aviator called Waldo Waterman successfully flew his Aerobile, the first true flying car.

It flew at 110 mph, drove at 55 mph, and only needed a small space to take off and land. Not a bad start. But development since then has been incredibly slow. Instead of wasting their time creating five-bladed bloody razors, inventors should be putting all their efforts into figuring out the best way to fit a pair of retractable wings onto a Mondeo.

DOLLY'S DOUBLE

You might think that sheep all look the same anyway, but Dolly really was *identical* – she was the first mammal ever to be cloned from an adult cell. And it happened today in 1997.

This famous breakthrough made the scientists at the Roslin Institute very happy – especially as they had tried to create 277 other clones before Dolly.

For the rest of us, Dolly's birth is worth cheering because she increased the possibility that in the future it will be possible to reproduce long-dead species such as woolly mammoths and even dinosaurs, *Jurassic Park*-style.

Incidentally, boffins named Dolly after curvy country singer Dolly Parton – because the cell for the cloning came from a mammary gland. They don't get out much, those boffins.

EDDIE 'THE EAGLE' SOARS

When Eddie Edwards took to the runway of the 90m Olympic ski jump on this day in 1988, his utter , utter hopelessness delighted the world. Here was a man who really had absolutely no chance: he was a stone and a half too heavy; his bottle-end glasses kept misting up (effectively blinding him); and he'd had to train himself.

But Eddie's charm lay not in the fact that he finished last; athletes do that every day. Nor was it just that he finished last by a very long way – almost fifty metres. The real delight lay in seeing a man who must have known *for a fact* that he wouldn't win but still put absolutely every ounce of his effort into trying.

Now, that's a proper bulldog spirit.

LAST INVASION OF BRITAIN

Today in 1797, in the name of freedom, we thank the brave actions of a band of 500 Welsh villagers who forced the surrender of the last invading force to land on British soil.

The mission was organised by revolutionary France, but has to go down in history as one of the most comically bad invasions ever mounted. Four warships planned to enter the port of Fishguard and move swiftly on Bristol. But they couldn't get into the harbour, and were forced to land miles away at an isolated outcrop. The invaders themselves were mostly conscripted convicts and prisoners of war who legged it as soon as they landed. The local militia and some boisterous farmers dealt with the rest.

All in all a bit shambolic, thankfully, otherwise we'd all be speaking French.

CHATEAU MARMONT

If headlong hedonism is what cheers you up, then Chateau Marmont is the place to head to today – when its swinging doors first opened as a hotel.

Harry Cohn, founder of Columbia Pictures, once said: 'If you are going to get in trouble, do it at the Chateau Marmont', and plenty of people listened. Jim Morrison of The Doors took getting high to a new level when he dangled from a drainpipe trying to swing from the roof into his hotel room and Led Zeppelin famously gunned their motorcycles through the lobby as guests cheered them on. If rock 'n' roll is a place, then this is it.

FIRST VOLKSWAGEN

Although the first Volkswagen factory was founded by a certain Mr Adolf Hitler, the company wouldn't exist today if it weren't for a British Army officer, Major Ivan Hirst. Today in April 1945, the American Army captured the bomb-damaged factory, but thought it was only fit for levelling. Major Hirst disagreed. Since the occupying forces were short of transport, he persuaded them to order 20,000 cars. By 1946, 1,000 cars a month were rolling off the production lines and the factory was on its way to becoming a leading part of the German economic recovery.

BYRON'S HOUSE OF LORDS ADDRESS

Sounds like a pretty cheerless thing to be commemorating, but Lord Byron was a uniquely controversial character who was tremendously entertaining to have around.

The speech he gave in the Lords on this day in 1812 for instance, which defended Luddite violence *against* the progress of the Industrial Revolution – must have absolutely charmed the upper house. In his life, Byron became a superstar poet and bedded dozens of the most beautiful aristocratic women in England and Europe. Although born with a clubfoot he managed to swim the tumultuous waters of the

Hellespont. He kept a pet bear when studying at Oxford and died as a hero of the Greek revolution.

And show me a man who wouldn't like to be called 'mad, bad and dangerous to know' and I'll show you a cheerless liar.

NYLON

Of all the fabrics that stockings were made of in 1935, silk was the most beautiful but also the most hideously expensive. Then on 28 February a brilliant chemist called Wallace Carothers produced half an ounce of a new polymer – Nylon – and put beautiful-looking legs within every woman's reach.

Nylon stockings made their debut, modelled by the suitably titled 'Miss Chemistry', at the New York World's Fair in 1939 and were an instant phenomenon. Although they are worn more rarely today, their impact on culture and fashion was profound: female leg-shaving became popular because the sheerness of the nylon stocking demanded ultra-smooth skin. Men rejoice!

LEAP DAY (NEXT IS 2012)

It's a bonus day – a whole extra day in the year – what possible reason can you have *not* to be cheerful?

Okay, so maybe you're at work. But today really is special – it only exists because the earth does not take exactly 365 days to go around the sun. A year is actually 365 days and six hours long. So after four years, an extra twenty-four hours have stacked up, and we add a day into the calendar.

And since it isn't exactly six hours extra, but five hours and forty nine minutes, some further time-bending is needed. But by the time you've worked all this out, the day has been wasted, so my advice is to put the book down and go and enjoy the day.

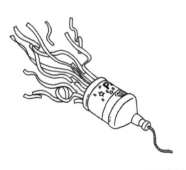

MARCH

YELLOWSTONE NATIONAL PARK

Nature's beauty always lifts the heart, and Yellowstone, with its spectacular gorges, serene lakes and abundant wildlife is certainly beautiful. The fact that Yellowstone was preserved by statute on this day in 1872 is particularly important as it established the first template for future national parks the world over.

We should also be cheerful today that the park hasn't been completely atomised. That's because the source of Yellowstone's beautifully bubbling thermal streams is a supervolcano forty miles in diameter. If it goes off, it would wipe out sixty per cent of life in North America and send the planet into another ice age.

THE COMPACT DISC

As well as being better quality than tapes, more convenient than records and harder to scratch, CDs are also worth celebrating for being one of the few products shown on *Tomorrow's World* that actually became reality.

The technology was first publicly demonstrated on the show way back in 1981 when Kieran Prendiville played a Bee Gees CD and spread jam all over it to demonstrate its indestructibility. Then on this day in 1983, the players themselves and sixteen discs were released. In the world of digital audio, this was very much the 'Big Bang' and a revolutionary day when music and superior technology fused.

WAR CAMELS

Hannibal had his war elephants, but a chap called Jefferson Davis had a far more entertaining battle-animal strategy – the US Camel Military Corps.

As US Secretary of War in 1855, Jefferson faced severe problems supplying troops in the far west. It was also difficult reconnoitring such wild terrain. So today he persuaded US Congress to give him $30,000 to get seventy seven camels shipped over from the Middle East. Alas, Jefferson's grand plan to use the beasts in battle (presumably to distract the enemy with laughter) never came to pass. The US

Civil War was on the horizon, and the Camel Corps was disbanded to move money elsewhere.

This was terrific news for the camels, who would have inevitably been useless in a fight against a gun.

CHERRY BLOSSOM FESTIVAL

 Clouds of pink and white cherry blossom have the power to take your breath away. Their beauty brightens many cities around the world, but particularly Vancouver, which has more than 36,000 trees and a Cherry Blossom Festival (which starts today) that's guaranteed to cheer you up.

The blossom is one of the first signs of spring, and the arrival of the flowers kick-starts a major cultural event. This features poetry, art, music, photography, and other cultural celebrations of the new season. Kids paint cherry blossom pictures, families walk and cycle along the cherry avenues, grown men sit beneath the boughs and read haiku to each other.

A few adventurous young lovers might even pop a cherry or two.

ST PIRAN'S DAY

A Cornish pasty is one of those cheering comfort foods that you'd enjoy an awful lot more frequently if you could just get the thought of all those calories and saturated fats out of your head. Well, forget your arteries for a moment, because today is St Piran's Day, the national day of the people of Cornwall – and the perfect excuse to treat yourself to a nice meaty pasty.

A traditional Cornish pasty is a half-moon of pastry with a crimped crust, filled with chopped steak, onion, swede and potato. The crust is important because it traditionally allowed Cornish tin miners to hold their lunch with mucky hands. When they'd eaten the meaty bit they could simple toss the grubby crust away.

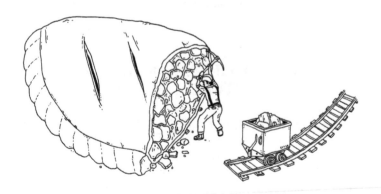

NATIONAL FROZEN FOOD DAY

6

If you've arrived home starving and found your fridge empty only to discover a pizza you'd forgotten about in the freezer compartment then today you can pay happy homage to Clarence Birdseye, father of frozen food.

Contrary to his TV adverts, Birdseye wasn't really a jolly old bearded sailor who knew a suspiciously large number of children. He actually started out as a naturalist for the US government. Posted to Labrador, Canada, Birdseye learned ice fishing from the Inuit. He also noticed that the -40°C temperatures froze his catch almost instantly, and yet tasted perfectly fresh when it thawed out. It took him years of finger-numbing research to perfect the fast-freezing technology, but eventually, in 1930, his frozen meat and veg made it into shops.

GOLDIE THE EAGLE EVADES
CAPTURE ... AGAIN

A golden eagle hunting among the serene boating ponds of Regent's Park is not something you see everyday, and today in 1965 it provided fantastic entertainment for the crowd which watched keepers, police, firefighters and a BBC reporter, completely fail to catch the restless raptor.

The imaginatively named Goldie found freedom when a keeper left his cage door open, and for twelve days had a great time on the loose in the park. He started off by scoffing a Muscovy duck in the American ambassador's garden and nearly carried off a couple of Cairn terriers. He then winged his way up to the West End to astonish the tourists in Tottenham Court Road. He was finally caught hanging around the wild fowl sanctuary, when he was lured with a dead rabbit.

MARDI GRAS (NEXT IN 2011)

Mardi Gras (from the French for 'fat Tuesday') is the last day of the three-day festival that precedes the traditional start of the forty days of Lent. (Although in many cultures the whole three-day period is now known as Mardi Gras, or Carnival.)

Roman Catholics are traditionally meant to abstain from all bodily pleasures during Lent, including eating meat. Carnival is therefore a handy way to bank forty days' worth of that sort of thing before Lent starts. However, these days, Mardi Gras now epitomises carnage, mayhem and three-day long parties. Not exactly what Catholics had in mind, but cheering nonetheless.

BARBIE'S DEBUT

Today is the day that millions of little girls around the world will cherish forever. It's the day Barbie rolled off the production line for the first time. In 1959, most dolls resembled the age of the children who played with them. But Ruth Handler realised that little girls like to play at being big girls, so she designed a doll with curves. Handily, Ruth's husband Elliot was a co-founder of the Mattel company, which makes plastic toys, and the rest is simply toy history.

Barbie has taken a lot of flak over the past half century for the physical role model she presents to children. If Barbie were real, she would be six feet tall, weigh 100lbs, and wear a dress size four. Her measurements would be 39-21-33. You don't see many Ken's complaining.

THE FIRST TELEPHONE CALL

The telephone had a humble start: all Alexander Graham Bell could think of to say in the *first ever* call, today in 1876, was 'Mr. Watson, come here, I want to see you'. Of course, these days, now you can check Facebook, find the nearest Starbucks, order your shopping from Tesco and watch videos of people falling over, all while listening to mp3s. What progress.

Bell offered to sell his patent to Western Union for $100,000.

The president of the telegraph company famously declined, saying the telephone was only a toy. A couple of years later he was heard to remark that if he could buy it for $25 million he would consider it a bargain. Bell, of course, didn't fancy selling it by this time.

MEXICO CONQUERED

Mars bars, pizzas, ice cream, chilli con carne and Bernard Matthews turkey twizzlers – if it hadn't been for Spaniard Hernàn Cortes, you wouldn't be able to enjoy any of these wonderfully delicious foods.

That's because chocolate, tomatoes, vanilla, turkey and chillies didn't exist in Europe until Hernàn Cortes brought them back from Mexico, which he conquered on this day in 1519. Of course, it wasn't such a cheerful day for the native Mexicans. They were conquered, for a start, and then in return for the wonderful bounty of their land, the invaders only gave them wheat, smallpox and measles. And Christianity.

THE 'PERFECT' DEAL

If you ever get a dose of the wonderful luck that Irene Motta got today in 1954, you should head straight for the nearest casino and bet your life away.

Irene was hosting a game of bridge when each of the four players turned up their hand to see thirteen cards of a single suit staring back at them. The odds against this happening are a rather large 2,235,197,406,895, 366,368,301,599,999 to 1. Which is roughly the same as tossing a coin ninety one times in a row and having it land heads every time.

We don't know if Irene did read any greater meaning into this unlikely happening. But she did okay in that particular game of bridge: she bid seven hearts and won the bid.

THE STORY OF EARMUFFS

Okay, so 99% of earmuffs are worn by twelve-year-old-girls, but what's cheering about today's tale is that they were invented by a fifteen-year-old boy.

On a very wintry day in 1873, Chester Greenwood headed out skating. It was so bitterly cold that he was soon heading back home again, with some seriously icy lugs. But he also had an idea. He built a pair of insulated pads lined with beaver fur and black velvet and linked them with a loop of wire. He stuck the contraption on his head and popped out skating again. Hey presto! – warm ears.

Chester patented the 'Champion Ear Protector' today in 1877 and by 1936 he had a factory producing 400,000 pairs a year.

Not bad for a schoolboy with big ears.

iLENSES

The concept of contact lenses is quite old: Leonardo da Vinci even suggested the idea back in the sixteenth century. But his plan was to submerge the eye in a bowl of water. Not that practical.

Then on this day in 1888 a German physiologist called Adolf Fick successfully fitted the first pair. They were made from heavy blown glass, were $\frac{3}{4}$ of an inch in diameter and could only be worn for a few hours at a time.

Scientists predict that the next step for contact lenses will be bionic implants impregnated with electronic circuits and infrared lights that generate a virtual display on the world around you. Prototypes have already been tested on rabbits – I kid you not.

GOOD CLEAN FUN

The Whirlpool bath was one of those happy accidents where a product turns out to have a much better use than the one it was designed for.

The Jacuzzi brothers originally made aircraft propellers and hydraulic pumps. One of the brothers, Candido, had a son with arthritis, and he was looking for a way to relieve the lad's pain. He had the light-bulb moment of fitting some of the company pumps into a bath. It worked, and Jacuzzi decided to sell the system as a therapeutic aid.

However, when Hollywood stars like Jayne Mansfield were pictured enjoying more than just therapy in one, the Jacuzzi soon became a sexy status symbol, and the thought of getting into one since has cheered many weary bones.

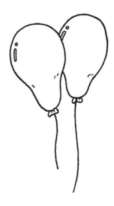

BACCHANALIA

One of the most fun things about the ancient Roman religion was that being devout wasn't dull. You simply worshipped Bacchus, the god of wine and theatre – because the Bacchanals held in his honour were some of the weirdest and wildest revels the world has ever seen.

Bacchanals took place in dark, labyrinthine groves, far from civilised parts of town. Strange games were played and severe forfeits taken from anyone not abiding by the rules. Drink flowed freely through the night, fuelling random sexual encounters. Worshippers often became so absorbed in their pleasure-seeking that it was many days before they found their way out.

In one of life's neat little coincidences, Las Vegas also became an incorporated city on this day in 1911. Just remember, whatever happens in Bacchanalia, stays in Bacchanalia.

ST PATRICK'S DAY

With its parades, performers and full-on party atmosphere, St Patrick's Day is clearly a day to make you cheerful. Particularly if you own shares in Guinness.

However, it's not immediately obvious why the humble, pious life of a fifth century shepherd is now commemorated by drunken street parties, dyed-green rivers and people dressed up (or is that down?) as leprechauns, but hey, any excuse for a good hose-up. Today is really just about celebrating Irishness and while there's nothing wrong with that, it's interesting to wonder what St Patrick himself would have made of all the nationalistic fervour; he was born in England, after all.

THE BEGINNING OF THE END FOR APARTHEID

For millions of South Africans and human rights advocates the world over, today is very much a day worth celebrating – in 1993 white South Africans voted for the political reforms that would end the racist apartheid regime and create a power-sharing multi-racial government.

A year later, F. W. de Klerk and Nelson Mandela were jointly awarded the Nobel Peace Prize. A general election was held on 27 April 1994 with the African National Congress (ANC) winning over sixty two per cent of the vote, and on 10 May, Mandela was sworn in as South Africa's president.

THE FUN IS IN TENTS

There's a simple, humble joy to be had from sleeping in a tent. After all, humans have been living under canvas much longer than they've been living in terraced houses.

You are at one with nature. You can hear the rain, feel the wind and dewy grass under your feet. You'll see the Milky Way scattered across the sky like icing sugar. And if you're camping somewhere really remote, you can add to the fun by lighting a fire – one of life's simplest, time-honoured pleasures.

So today, as most of the campsites around the country open for the new camping season, why not dust off your old Force Ten? You might just be opening up a whole field of fun.

ZIPPERY-DOO-DAH-ZIPPERY-DAY

All over the world, people desperate for the loo give thanks today to Gideon Sundback, inventor of the modern zip. It was patented on this day, in 1917.

Sundback truly understood the plight of the modern man who'd had six pints on a cold night and from 1906 to 1917 he dedicated his life (imagine that?) to perfecting the quick-opening front-trouser fastener.

The one major downside to Sundback's invention, of course, is that no one ever snagged their foreskin in a set of buttons. Brings a tear to the eye just thinking about that . . .

WORLD POETRY DAY

For lots of people poetry means being bored to sleep by an English teacher with patches on his elbows waffling on about Wordsworth. Which is a shame, because poetry can be uplifting, moving and completely hilarious (yes, mucky limericks do count as poetry). And today was set aside by UNESCO in 1999 as just the day for getting some of that poetic joy back into your life.

LASER QUEST

Whether it's correcting your eyesight, playing DVDs, adding up your supermarket shopping or blowing away bad guys in sci-fi movies, the laser is *the* futuristic invention of the 20th century. And on this day in 1960 inventors Arthur Schawlow and Charles Townes picked up the patent.

Laser was initially coined as an acronym meaning Light

Amplification By Stimulated Emission of Radiation but the term stuck. It's an invention that has had thousands of practical uses that were never originally predicted by its discoverers. Think about it. If you actually sat down and tried to come up with a form of radiation that would both improve missile guidance systems *and* treat zits, you probably wouldn't get very far.

OTIS' SAFETY ELEVATOR

Elisha Otis has perhaps had more influence on the shape of modern cities than any other person. For centuries, there had been freight hoists and even primitive passenger elevators, but they worked using a rope-and-pulley system, and if the rope broke, you were dead. It wasn't until 1853's New York World Fair, that, standing on an elevator platform of his own design, he ordered the only rope holding him up to be cut. A nervous axeman obeyed, and to the gasps of the collected crowd, the platform dropped just a few inches before this showboating inventor's pioneering safety mechanism held strong.

The modern elevator had arrived, ushering in the era when buildings could stretch to previously unimagined heights.

TEA BAG FIRST DIPPED

Relaxing with a cuppa is the perfect way to lift your spirits – so stick the kettle on, put your feet up and break open a new packet of Hob Nobs . . . today we celebrate the mighty tea bag.

Surprisingly for such a quintessentially English tradition, the tea bag was patented by an American, on this day in 1908. A tea dealer called Thomas Sullivan was thinking of ways to save money when he had the notion of sending out his tea samples in small silk pouches rather than the then-common tin cans. Many of his potential customers were confused by these little packages and popped them into a mug with some hot water, thereby accidentally inventing the modern tea bag.

SKIING ON HAMPSTEAD HEATH

Imagine the delight on the faces of dog walkers and schoolchildren when, on a *warm* March day in 1950, they encountered a nearly full-size ski jump, with real snow and skiers . . . on Hampstead Heath.

Visitors to London's famous heathland might have thought they had taken a wrong turn and ended up in Norway, and in a way they had: that's where all the snow and most of the skiers were imported from. The Norwegian jumpers simply brought forty five tons of snow with them, packed in wooden boxes insulated by dry ice. The jump itself was constructed locally, with a 100-foot-take-off ramp that launched jumpers ninety feet down the heath.

THE FIRST DRIVING TEST

You may think it's not something to be cheerful about but the driving test has definitely made the world a safer place.

In the early twentieth century, cars developed far faster than drivers' skills, knocking over 7,000 unfortunate people a year. Then on this day in 1934 the Minister of Transport, Leslie Hore-Belisha (of beacon fame), laid down a new law. There were no test centres so candidates had to meet their examiners on street corners. It sounds a bit sordid, but it worked. Within a year, the number of fatalities had fallen by nearly 1,000.

And cheerfully enough, the very first person to pass the basic half-hour test of driving skills and knowledge of the Highway Code was a chap called Mr Beene.

VIAGRA RISES TO PROMINENCE

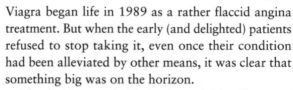

Viagra began life in 1989 as a rather flaccid angina treatment. But when the early (and delighted) patients refused to stop taking it, even once their condition had been alleviated by other means, it was clear that something big was on the horizon.

The drug's remarkable unplanned side-effect soon became its *raison d'être* and it quickly rose to fame. Within fourteen days of today – its official launch – and despite a high price, US doctors were prescribing Viagra more than 110,000 times a week for erectile dysfunction. Just three months later, two million Viagra prescriptions had been written in the US alone and the Little Blue Pill had a rock-solid reputation both as a chemical aphrodisiac and club culture's latest must-try drug.

ALKA SELTZER

Alka Seltzer may be one of the very few hangover 'cures' that actually does some good. Its bicarbonate and citric acid react with water to produce carbon dioxide gas that settles your stomach and helps you ingest the aspirin, which sorts out the throbbing pain in your head.

Launched by the Bayer Corporation today in 1931, it was first sold as a cure for practically everything – including an ailment Bayer called 'The Blahs'. That might seem irresponsible, until you remember that the Bayer Corporation also invented heroin, which they sold as a cough medicine until 1910.

IRELAND STUBS IT OUT

Smoking bans make non-smokers and health campaigners very cheerful indeed, and on this day in 2004 Ireland became the first country to outlaw smoking in all work places, bars and restaurants.

Of course, being forced to stand outside in the sheeting rain makes smokers less than cheerful, but the theory is that they'll be healthier in the long term. In Montana, USA, where a similar ban was introduced, a study found a forty per cent reduction in heart attacks following the imposition of a smoking ban. Another study noted a twelve per cent drop in bar workers' phlegm production, although how they measured that one, you really don't want to know.

FIRST GENERAL ANAESTHESIA

Before anaesthetic, surgery was more like medieval torture than any modern medical procedure. Your only anaesthetic option was to don a leather helmet and have the surgeon smack you on the head with a mallet. Then today in 1842 Dr Crawford Long knocked a patient out with ether and removed a cyst from his neck.

Like many medical students in the 1830s, Long had horsed around with ether at parties, inhaling it from balloons and enjoying its narcotic effects. When he later became Dr Long in a small-town practice, he remembered how he had never felt any of the bumps and bruises he gathered while under ether's influence – and ended the days of indescribable pain while undergoing life-saving surgery.

THE EIFFEL TOWER INAUGURATION

Thrusting over a thousand feet into the Parisian sky, the Eiffel Tower is the world's most recognisable phallus, sorry, building.

Gustave Eiffel originally intended it to be erected in Barcelona, but he failed to arouse much interest.

But its sexual shape was clearly behind much of the 'eyesore' criticisms levelled at it by locals when it was inaugurated today in 1889. Parisians considered it ugly and looked forward to its removal – scheduled for 1909. Attitudes changed over the years and its deconstruction plans were forgotten. It's now one of the most popular tourist attractions in the world and an instantly recognisable symbol of Paris.

APRIL

APRIL FOOLS' DAY

Playing tricks on people is a great way to cheer yourself up, and today is the one day when the whole world enjoys a joke.

In 1698, several people were tricked by an advert into going to the Tower of London to 'see the lions washed'. In 1962, thousands of Swedes fell for a TV report explaining how they could get colour on a black and white set by stretching a nylon stocking over the screen. While Sir Patrick Moore once told radio listeners in 1976 that a unique planetary alignment would affect gravity, and he asked them to jump in the air at exactly 9.47a.m. to experience 'a strange floating sensation.' The switchboard was jammed with 'fools' claiming it had worked.

KANAMARA PENIS FESTIVAL

Penises are funny-looking things anyway, but if they're ten feet long, being carried on the shoulders of twelve rhythmically chanting men coming down a Japanese street, you really do have to smile.

The Kanamara shrine in Kawasaki hosts all the action today; the story goes that prostitutes used to pray here for protection against sexually transmitted diseases. The event grew into a spring fertility festival but now it's wall-to-wall willies. Kids carve members from radishes, transvestites line the streets and respectable old ladies giggle as they suck penis-shaped lollipops. It's not something you can imagine happening at your local church hall fête but it's all in good fun.

If this hasn't aroused your interest, don't worry, National Cleavage Day (7 April) is just around the corner.

WORLD PARTY DAY

That all the world's problems can be solved if everyone just got a bit drunk and had a laugh with their friends is a philosophical concept that has occurred to everyone who has got a bit drunk and had a laugh with their friends. So today is tremendously important in that it gives us a chance to test this hypothesis.

World Party Day started off as a fictional concept in the 1995 novel *Flight* by Vanna Bonta. The basic idea is that the opposite of war is not peace, but party. And thus a World Party is the opposite of a World War.

So get some friends together today and start saving civilisation!

FRED AND GINGER'S LAST DANCE

Fred Astaire and Ginger Rogers made ten very cheerful films together, and *The Barkleys of Broadway* that premiered today in 1949 was their last. It was also the only colour film they ever appeared in.

As with many successful artists, it took a while before the powers that be realised the magic they had in their hands. Hollywood folklore relates that the feedback on Fred's first screen test read: 'Can't sing. Can't act. Balding. Can dance a little'.

BIRKENHEAD PARK OPENS

The Wirral might not spring to mind as the most wondrous of natural environments to be celebrating today, but its park has given the world a lot to be cheerful about.

Birkenhead Park boasts acres of landscaped lawns,

lakes, trees, flower beds and winding paths. It was Britain's first publicly-funded civic park when it opened on this day in 1847, and it influenced many other beauty spots across the UK.

And this garden of earthly delights so thrilled the American landscape architect Frederick Law Olmsted, that he paid it the ultimate compliment by replicating its features for his own landscaping masterpiece – Central Park, New York.

TARTAN DAY

If you like the feel of a brisk wind around your sporran, then today's your McDay. Tartan Day commemorates everything Scottish on the date when the Declaration of Arbroath, a powerful proclamation of Scotland's right to be independent, was signed in 1320.

The celebrations were actually started in the US in 1982, by the New York Caledonian Club. They organised a one-off celebration of the 200th Anniversary of the repeal of the Act of Proscription, the law that banned the wearing of tartan.

With swirling kilts, swaggering whisky drinkers, wall-to-wall Sean Connery impressions and the shrieking of bagpipes, Tartan Day gives those of Scots descent an excellent chance to remember why their ancestors left their homeland in the first place.

NATIONAL CLEAVAGE DAY

Here's a day that's way out in front when it comes to fun. National Cleavage Day is an annual celebration of ladies' boobs. The fun includes charity dinners, cocktail parties and 'Best Cleavage' competitions. The day is, not unsurprisingly, sponsored by Wonderbra.

Many women participating in the event say it gives them a chance to celebrate a part of their femininity that is usually only appreciated furtively. Other women claim that it is a cynical commercial exercise that uses sex as a marketing tool and gives men an excuse for ogling breasts all day.

At the moment the event is mostly celebrated in South Africa, but with a little bit of encouragement, we could probably ensure the fun spreads internationally. So please, give National Cleavage Day your full support.

HAPPY BIRTHDAY BUDDHA

One of the world's most peace-loving and joyful religions, Buddhism has brought spiritual cheer to millions of people for over 2,500 years.

Buddhists (around 350 million in the world today) focus on his teachings of peace, mindfulness and devotion. They believe that we should care for each other and the natural world around us – the earth, animals, birds, plants and insects. Buddhists will often be vegetarians and will refrain from drink, drugs and eating to excess. Quiet meditation is an important part of their spirituality.

Notable modern peace-loving Buddhists include Jackie Chan, Jet Li, Steven Seagal and Bruce Lee. Hmm . . .

THE HEFF

Smut magnate Hugh Hefner may not be wholly PC, but he's clearly far too busy having fun to give a damn what anyone thinks of him. Which is very cheering, if not a little enviable.

Born today in 1926, Hefner has been one of the all-time great party hosts and cheer-spreaders since he released his first, culture-baiting issue of *Playboy* in December 1953. His Playboy mansion remains the only private residence in the city of Los Angeles with permits for fireworks displays and a zoo. There is also rumoured to be a secret 'Elvis' room, where the King once spent the night with no less than eight girls.

On an unbelievable-but-true note, Hugh's mother hoped he was going to grow up to be a missionary. At least he's mastered the position of one...

PING-PONG DIPLOMACY

The world would be a lot cheerier if icy diplomatic relations could be thawed out with a spot of ping-pong. Unlikely? Well, that's exactly what happened today in 1971.

Mao Zedong was dictator of China and the US was fighting in Vietnam; relations between the countries were terrible. Meanwhile, the US Table Tennis team was in Japan for the World Championship when one of their players missed the team bus after a practice. Suddenly, a Chinese player offered him a ride on their bus and an unlikely friendship was born. A few days later, nine American players crossed from Hong Kong into China, bats in hand.

So much goodwill was generated by their visit that the next year, Richard Nixon became the first US president ever to visit communist China.

THE THEORY OF RELATIVITY

Einstein was the perfect eccentric professor – he smoked a pipe, had bonkers hair, talked to his cat and never wore socks. However, it was his Special Relativity theory, which he announced on this day in 1905, that propelled him to fame in the physics world and made him the public's genius of choice.

His famous equation $E = mc^2$ is one of the few scientific theories to have crossed over into mainstream culture even if most people don't actually understand what it represents and I won't even begin to try! Renowned relativity expert Arthur Eddington was asked if it was true that only three people (including Einstein) really understood Relativity, Eddington replied, 'I wonder, who is the third?'

THE START OF CEREALIA

Sloshing ice-cold milk on a crisp and delicious bowl of cereal is one of life's loveliest pleasures.

The ancient Romans were big on this too and set aside a whole week for a festival in honour of their goddess Ceres (it's from her that we get the word 'cereal'). She and her godly minions looked after the fertility of the soil with particular responsibility for grain-producing plants and on this day her loyal followers laid leafy offerings in her temple on Rome's Aventine Hill.

Quite what the ancient Romans would think of Coco Pops Crunchers however, is anyone's guess.

JAMES BOND DAY

The exact origins of the martini cocktail are for some reason a little fuzzy. But today we raise a 'shaken, not stirred' cheer to the man who so famously enjoyed them – James Bond, whose first adventure, *Casino Royale*, was published today in 1953.

In this book Bond actually drinks a 'Vesper': a cocktail of his own design named after the story's femme fatale. It comprises three measures of Gordon's Gin, one of vodka and half a measure of Kina Lillet, shaken until ice-cold and topped with a slice of lemon peel.

Bond's creator, Ian Fleming, used to drink a bottle of gin a day. When his doctor warned him about his failing health, he nodded gratefully and immediately switched to bourbon.

SEVEN MILLION TULIPS AT KEUKENHOF

If I say that Dutch plants can make you happy, you'll think I'm talking of the coffee shops of Amsterdam. But if you fancy a more natural 'high', then Keukenhof, the world's largest flower garden is the place to be today.

It starts the week when the tulips blossom most beautifully, and here you can wander past millions and millions of blooms. Your senses will sing and your heart will soar with good cheer – naturally.

Because there's actual scientific proof that flowers make you cheerful. A study by the State University of New Jersey found that people who received flowers felt measurably more positive than subjects who didn't. And if the Keukenhof doesn't do the trick, Amsterdam is not that far away.

BRITAIN HONOURS A FOREIGN HERO

Sometimes someone steps up in the face of chaos and does something so unselfishly brave that it thrills the heart – like Reis Leming, a young American airman.

The east coast floods of January 1953 were savage. Hurricane-force-smashed into East Anglia devastating entire towns. From the screaming wind and rain, Reis knew things were very serious. But rather than lock himself in for safety, he got hold of a tiny rubber raft and paddled out into the pitch-black ferocity. He worked for hours in the teeth of the gale, rescuing terrified survivors from rooftops until he collapsed with severe hypothermia.

Reis recovered, and today in 1953 he became the first foreigner to receive the George Medal in peacetime. And boy did he deserve it: the twenty-two-year old lad in his little rubber boat saved the lives of twenty seven people.

THE BIRTH OF CHARLIE CHAPLIN

Born in 1889, today the world celebrates the life of Charles Chaplin. Throughout the tough times of World War I, the Great Depression, the rise of Fascism and World War II, Charlie Chaplin was acting, writing, directing, producing and scoring films that united the entire world in laughter. No small feat.

For a laugh, Chaplin once entered a 'Chaplin look-alike' competition. He came third.

THE WAR ENDS ... AFTER 335 YEARS

For the residents of the Isles of Scilly (otherwise known as Scillonians), today in 1986 brought an end to more than three centuries of perpetual fear.

In 1648, Oliver Cromwell was winning the Civil War and his forces had pushed the Royalists to the very edges of England. His Dutch allies sailed to Scilly to harass the remains of the Royalist navy. The locals told them to 'clog off' and so the Netherlands declared war on the islands. Shortly after, the Royalist fleet was forced to surrender. The Dutch then departed in safety, and the whole war thing seemed so obscure that no one officially declared peace.

Harmony was finally established 335 years later at a more jovial gathering on Scilly. The Dutch Ambassador joked that it must have been harrowing 'to know we could have attacked at any moment'.

NO NEWS DAY

It's clear that some days are slow-news days. But rather than admit this, news services just promote less important items into headline news.

Unless of course, you're BBC Radio today in 1930. In that case, you are refreshingly, decently, cheerfully, honest about the lack of anything worth reporting. That's why listeners tuning in on Easter Friday to find out what was going on in the world heard the following announcement: 'Good Evening. Today is Good Friday. There is no news.'

Some piano music then played.

LSD BICYCLE TRIP DAY

On this day in 1943, Dr Albert Hofmann not only became the first person in the world to synthesise lysergic acid diethylamide (LSD), he also became the first to experience a full-blown acid trip . . . and then get on his bike.

At first he ingested the drug by accident through his fingertips. This small taster inspired him to self-administer a proper dose. The effects of this were slow acting, and the good doctor had set off home on his bicycle when he really started to wig out. It's this famous hallucinogenic ride that is commemorated today by acid fans around the world.

Hofmann remained a supporter of the benefits of psychedelic substances throughout his life. This greatly annoyed many anti-drug officials, since the doctor was passionate, erudite and lived to the grand old age of 102.

VITAPHONE AND THE TALKIES

Movies with ear-splitting Dolby surround sound are now so commonplace that it's easy to forget that once upon a time movies had no sound at all.

Early attempts at 'talkies' made the actors sound like they were jammed in a small tin box. However, on this day in 1926 the pioneering Vitaphone technology was released by Warner Bros. The system was basically a sixteen-inch phonograph record that held the soundtrack separately and then played along with the film – hopefully in sync.

It was loud, proud and sounded brilliant, and the first feature using Vitaphone (*The Jazz Singer, 1927*) was so successful that cinema adopted the technology for all releases.

ROSIE RUIZ VIVAS WINS THE BOSTON MARATHON ... SORT OF

Rosie Ruiz really wanted to win the Boston Marathon. And she wasn't going to let the fact that she couldn't run particularly fast get in the way of that dream. So she hatched a plan: register for the race, hide in the crowd a mile from the finish and just before the leading runners come past, leap into the race and belt for the finish.

Daft? Well, it worked. Today in 1980, Rosie won the Boston Marathon in a record of two hours, thirty one minutes and fifty six seconds – three whole minutes ahead of second place. She got the winner's medal and made all the headlines. Then officials started asking questions: Why had no one seen her in the earlier stages of the race? Why wasn't she exhausted?

Eventually the penny dropped.

Not that we want to celebrate cheating, but the sheer barefaced brilliance of Rosie's 'cunning plan' always makes me smile, even if she was stripped of her medals and make into a public disgrace.

EARTH DAY

 Earth Day was the idea of Gaylord Nelson, a US senator who was shocked into action by an oil spill in Santa Barbara in 1969. Spreading the word through high schools across the country, he moved more than twenty million Americans to take peaceful action in the name of the environment on this day in 1970. Thanks to Earth Day, the US subsequently introduced the Clean Air Act and was single-handedly responsible for creating the Environmental Protection Agency a year later.

Earth Day is currently observed in 175 countries, and is claimed to be the largest secular holiday in the world, with more than half a billion people celebrating the continuing protection of our planet every year.

WORLD BOOK DAY

Curling up with a cup of tea and a good book is guaranteed to soothe the soul. And seeing as it's World Book Day today is the perfect time to do just that.

Today has been chosen because two of the world's greatest writers, Miguel de Cervantes and William Shakespeare both died on this day in 1616. Even more handily, Shakespeare was also born on this day.

Talking of deathbeds, Shakespeare seems to have been remarkably cheerful while on his. In his will he took great care to barely mention his wife Anne, the mother of his three children, except to specify that she received 'my second best bed'.

What a charmer.

TROJANS 0, GREEKS 1

The Trojan horse debacle led to a very cheerful day for the ancient Greeks and it offers a bit of fun for the rest of us – the only unhappy people were the Trojans themselves, but they were so monumentally stupid that they deserved everything they got.

Imagine you're a Trojan for one minute. The entire Greek army is camped outside the gates of Troy, your home city. They're absolutely desperate to destroy your entire way of life, but you have frustrated their every effort for ten long years. Then, out of the blue, they start building an absolutely gigantic wooden horse.

Hmmm.

No sooner have they finished this enormous equine edifice than they apparently sail away, completely forgetting to take it with them.

Double hmmm.

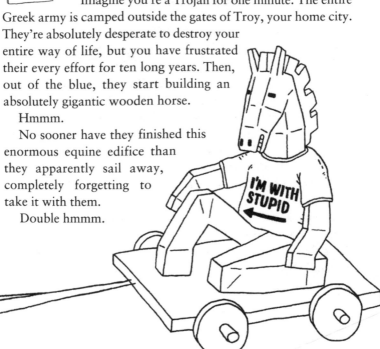

Now, there are clearly many options to be considered, and not everyone is an expert military strategist, but it should be pretty clear that *at no point whatsoever* should you tow the horse into the city, get pissed and go to bed.

See what I mean? Idiots.

DNA DECODED

 The discovery of the structure of DNA (Deoxyribose Nucleic Acid) has led to incredible advances in biotechnology and medicine.

DNA makes up the genes that pass on our hereditary characteristics. Your dad's got a big nose? Thanks to DNA, so do you. But its exact structure had long baffled the biggest brains in biology. Then, after years of forehead rubbing and chin scratching, two Cambridge University scientists, James Watson and Francis Crick, finally worked out today in 1953 that DNA was structured as a double helix, or two spirals linked together.

Watson and Crick were so excited at their discovery that they promptly went to the pub, announcing to the regulars in the Eagle that, 'We have found the secret of life!' They might have been talking about the bar's IPA, not DNA, but either way, it's a good line.

SUNDAY SPORTS
(AUTHORISED BY QUEEN ELIZABETH)

If it weren't for Queen Elizabeth I's laid-back law-making, you may have been forced to do more DIY this weekend instead of kicking back and watching the footie . . .

Perhaps influenced by sixteenth century publicans, good Queen Bess passed a decree today in 1569 explicitly allowing Sunday sports. Where men had previously been forced to go to church and . . . go to church again, they were now at full liberty to enjoy 'shooting with the broad arrow, the shooting at twelve score prick, the shooting at the Turk, the leaping for men, the running for men, the wrestling, the throwing of the sledge, and the pitching of the bar'.

All of which sounds mad, but a lot more fun than going to church.

BETTY BOOTHROYD

Politics is stuffy at the best of times, so it cheered the spirits no end when Betty Boothroyd became the first-ever female Speaker in parliament's 700-year history on this day in 1992.

It wasn't just the fact that she was a woman. In her youth, Betty had been a dancer with the Tiller Girls, a troupe famous for their high-kicking routines, and she brought the same boldness and glamour to her new role. She immediately dispensed with the ridiculous tradition of the Speaker's wig and took no nonsense from the MPs – she brought her first 'Prime Minister's Questions' to an end by barking, 'Right – time's up!' at the astonished House.

ELY EEL DAY

Just because life deals you a duff hand, doesn't mean you can't be cheerful. Take the people of Ely, Cambridgeshire. Their town lies low in a marsh and is named after one of the world's least attractive fish, the eel. But every year the residents rise above their damp surroundings by celebrating the Ely Eel Day.

You can buy paintings of eels at a craft stall, sing about eels on the music stage or eat eels in the food tent. But the undisputed highlight of the day is the . . . wait for it . . . eel-throwing competition. Of course, since an eel is almost impossible to hold, let alone throw, you actually toss some socks rolled into a pair of tights instead.

Not as fun, obviously, but less likely to get you in trouble with the RSPCA.

WELCOME TO BUCKINGHAM PALACE

Windsor Castle was unfortunately gutted by fire in 1992, so on this day in 1993, the Queen decided to throw open the gold-adorned doors of her 'gaff' to any common-or-garden pleb who had £17 to spend on looking at a bunch of paintings and furniture.

Disappointingly, though, visitors could only see a selection of state rooms – nobody was allowed to view the fun rooms where all the majestic magic happens. I mean, I can't be the only weirdo who would like to see what books Her Majesty keeps by the loo?

I'm betting it's not this one . . .

BELTANE EVE

This Gaelic festival traditionally celebrated the first day of summer in Ireland, Scotland and the Isle of Man. However, if you just fancy a bit of neo-pagan partying today then head to Edinburgh – it has hosted the Beltane Fire Festival since 1988. This wild and wonderful gathering of cavorting Celts, fire dancers and passing hedonists runs through the night of 30 April on Calton Hill in the city centre, and draws 15,000 people annually.

MAY

POSTAGE, LICKED

 Email is all very well, but there's something very special about receiving an old-fashioned stamped letter. And if it comes from an admirer, well your heart practically sings. And that's only possible thanks to the lickably adhesive postage stamp which first appeared today in 1840.

Sir Rowland Hill introduced the idea as one of his postal reforms, and although it seems obvious now, it was radical at the time. Politicians called it 'preposterous' and doomed to failure. But the 'Penny Black' was an instant success when first sold, and the concept changed postal services around the world, sending mail volumes rocketing and helping businesses become more profitable.

Stamps are also low in calories too – one lick is just one tenth of a calorie!

LOCH NESS MONSTER ... SIGHTED

This day in 1933 saw the first modern newspaper report of a monster that had long been rumoured to lurk in the deep dark waters of Loch Ness.

The story raised some interest, but might have remained just a local curiosity, were it not for the Secretary of State for Scotland giving the local police a special order to prevent any attacks on the creature. And with that official nod, the public's interest was piqued. The next year the famous Surgeon's Photograph appeared. This was later agreed to be a fake, created from a toy submarine and a sock puppet, but the seed was sewn by then. Whether it exists or not, the Loch Ness Monster puts around £120 million a year into highland sporrans.

NAKED TWISTER DAY

The brilliant children's party game 'Twister' hit mainstream society tonight in 1966 when Eva Gabor played it with Johnny Carson on *The Tonight Show*. The adult version, 'Naked Twister', was conceived a nano-second later by the liberal American public.

If you lack the (very) good friends to play a saucy game with, head to the town of Duncanville, Texas. It boasts a split-level nightclub, the upper level of which is solely dedicated to playing 'Naked Twister' . . . every day of the year.

CHRISTOPHER COLUMBUS FINDS JAMAICA

Despite being a small island of less than three million people, Jamaicans with their predominantly positive outlook on life have given the world a lot to smile about. From Bob Marley and Reggae to copious amounts of rum – Jamaica is the place where everything is always 'irie'. And on this day, in 1494, after his second voyage to the New World, Mr Columbus declared that he had 'found' it. Of course, it was already there, but still, a good reason to be cheerful nonetheless.

CHANEL NO. 5

As fans of Brut 33 will tell you, fashions change in the world of fragrances. But Chanel No. 5 has bucked all trends and has probably made more women feel fragrantly feminine than any other perfume.

It may be a timeless classic now, but it was a very bold fragrance when launched today in 1922. Most perfumes of the time made women smell like Kew Gardens. Coco Chanel, however, sought something deliberately artificial, a composition 'like a dress'. The fragrance's legendary status was sealed in 1953 when Marilyn Monroe was asked what she wore in bed. She replied only with, 'Five drops of No. 5'.

INTERNATIONAL NO DIET DAY

Why not take advantage of the fact that today is International No Diet Day and tell Mr Atkins to F-Plan off.

Unless you're a masochist, going on a diet is a bloody miserable experience. And chances are, if you picked up this book about being cheerful, I doubt you are the kind of person who takes dieting that seriously. Yet everybody does it at some stage or another in their life. Usually on 2 January for a week or so. However, dieting does not make you slimmer in the long term – it is reckoned 83% of dieters eventually put more weight back on than they lose. So what's the point?

Most importantly of all, you are gorgeous just as you are.

NO PANTS DAY

No Pants Day started back in 1985 as a prank, but the partici . . . pants enjoyed it so much that they decided to get their kit off every year.

Why? because, apparently, when 'large groups of people parade in public without their pants, amazing things are bound to happen'. This is according to the good people at www.nopantsday.com.

It's worth pointing out that No Pants Day started in America, so if you're in the UK, it's your *trousers* you should be omitting.

Not wearing underpants isn't going to cause that much hilarity. Unless you don't wear trousers as well, but then the fun won't last for very long before the police arrive.

COCA-COLA FIRST SOLD

When it was first released on this day in 1886, Coca-Cola was decreed the most cheerful drink in the world. That's because a single serving had up to fifty milligrams of pure cocaine in it.

This recipe is not unexpected when you consider that Coke's inventor, John Pemberton, was himself a drug addict.

Cocaine was removed from Coke in 1903, but coca leaves are still used to flavour the drink. The cocaine is extracted first in a factory in New Jersey and the drug is then sold to a pharmaceutical company.

British cocaine fans weren't disappointed though – they could still buy the drug in Harrods until 1916.

NATIONAL TRAIN DAY

Rattling along in a beautifully liveried carriage pulled by a puffing engine is great fun, and not just for those old enough to remember steam trains running regularly.

It's National Train Day in the US, commemorating the completion of the first transcontinental railroad. As of this day in 1869, bandits could raid trains anywhere from the Pacific to the Atlantic while villains could tie damsels to more than 1,776 miles of track.

British train lovers can also celebrate the first appearance of Thomas the Tank Engine today, in the 1945 book *The Three Railway Engines*.

THE BIRTH OF KARAOKE

The best thing about karaoke is that the worse people are at it, the more fun it gives you. And on this day, the man who created this form of entertainment was born.

One day, back in the early 1970s, Japanese drummer Daisuke Inoue couldn't make it to a gig so he pre-taped a backing track. This went down well in Japan's after-dinner entertainment scene, so he built his own machine that played such tracks for a 100-yen coin – and karaoke was born. Today, Abba's 'Waterloo' is the most played karaoke tune in Britain.

OSCAR IS BORN

For actors and movie producers all over the world, give yourself another pat on the back today. It's a little known fact that Hollywood's Academy Awards only exist because Louis B. Mayer, the former head of MGM, wanted to create an organisation to mediate labour disputes. He soon realised that it could also promote the movie industry as a whole, and he held a banquet for all the industry bigwigs at which he pitched this idea. It got a big thumbs-up and on this day in 1927 the Oscar was born. The first glamorous Awards ceremony took place two years later.

INTERNATIONAL NURSES DAY

Nurses are one of those forces for good that we simply take for granted. So it's fitting that today we should celebrate their huge contribution to society on the birthday of the most famous nurse of all, Florence Nightingale, born in 1820.

'The Lady with the Lamp' wasn't just a soothing sight for wounded soldiers, she also laid the foundations for the entire nursing profession. Her book *Notes on Nursing* is a classic text; she was an early promoter of hygiene and sanitation; she established the world's first secular nursing school; and her trainees went into the workhouse system to care for the poor, heralding the era of the modern National Health Service.

MIRROR BALL, MIRROR BALL ON THE WALL

Strutting your stuff beneath the sparkling lights of a mirror ball is guaranteed to put us all in a cheerful mood, even if you can't quite cut the rug like John Travolta.

Although it was most popular in the disco scene of the 1970s, the mirrored ball actually appeared much, much earlier than that. It was glimpsed by the world at large for the first time in *Berlin: Symphony of a Great City,* a German silent film that was released today in 1928.

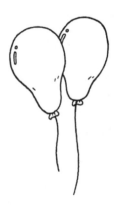

PULILAN CARABAO FESTIVAL

Taking pride in your job helps you feel good about yourself. And just because you tend water buffalo, doesn't mean you have to miss out on the fun – at least according to the farmers of Pulilan in the Philippines.

They love their hard-working water buffalo, or *carabao*, so much that every 14 May they spend two days treating the beasts like royalty. First, the farmers politely shave them, then soften their hides with oil and marinade them in perfume before decorating them with paint and ribbons. In the afternoon, they have a parade in the town square and bless them before a church. The next day, the groomed and preened buffalos compete in a race.

You can't see this happening in Swindon, can you?

FLAVOUR OF THE MONTH

Crisps, ironically, would be pretty boring if all they tasted of was potato. But that's all they *did* taste of, from when they first appeared in the mid-nineteenth century right up until 1954. So snack lovers everywhere should be very happy that Mr Joe 'Spud' Murphy, boss of Tayto, cooked up the first-ever batch of a new, revolutionary crisp flavouring today – Cheese and Onion.

Cheese and Onion has been a hit ever since and is actually getting *more* popular. In 2009, it finally eclipsed Ready Salted as Britain's No.1 flavour.

PRESCOTT PUNCHES PROTESTER

When Deputy Prime Minister John Prescott acted on instinct today in 2001 and punched a protester who threw an egg at him, it brightened up everyone's day.

It was great telly too. A line of protesters, held back by police, with Prescott walking in front of them. Then one demonstrator spots a gap, steps forward and lets the Deputy PM have a free ranger right in the face. An MP being egged is always good fun for starters, but Prescott's reaction – reassuringly human for a politician – was a cracking left jab to the cheek. Everyone was stunned. The guy who threw the egg had *the* most horrendous mullet, so he doubly deserved it.

FIRST WEEKLY COMIC

17 A weekly dose of comic cheer was always something to look forward to when you were a kid. And the very first regular chuckles appeared on this day in 1890, thanks to the title *Comic Cuts*, published by Alfred Harmsworth.

Comic Cuts' early issues were just rehashed stories knocked off from US publications without permission but the kids didn't care – they lapped up the cartoon laughs. The comic became hugely popular and established the format that would later be replicated by *The Dandy* and *The Beano*. Its style has also been parodied for lots of adult fun by comics such as *Viz*.

Alfred Harmsworth made so much money from his comics for kids, that he decided to launch comics for adults too – namely *The Daily Mail* and *The Daily Mirror*.

THE FIRST EVER LAWNMOWER

18 Your lawn wouldn't be quite as lovely a place to relax if it was covered in sheep poo, but that was pretty much how it had to be until this wonderful day in 1830.

Before then, 'lawns' were indistinguishable from meadows. They were either laboriously hand-cut by a scythe or naturally trimmed by animals. Then John Ferrabee and Edwin Budding of Gloucestershire went into business making the first mechanical lawnmowers and by doing so helped create the modern garden. For the first time, gardeners could close-crop a large area of lawn. Horticulture became a massive hobby soon after and sports such as tennis, croquet, golf and football boomed.

GUINNESS EXPORT

Arthur Guinness started his famous brewery in Dublin in 1759. Ten years later on this magical day, he shipped the first ever six-and-a-half barrels of ale to England – giving the English six-and-a-half reasons to be cheerful. Today, Guinness is Ireland's biggest global export.

As well as being tasty and full of alcohol, Guinness offers only 198 calories per pint – less than skimmed milk.

HOLIDAYS PACKAGED

The very first all-in flight-and-accommodation trip, or package holiday as we know it now, left Gatwick airport on this day in 1950 for Corsica. Vladimir Raitz, a Russian-born British businessman, had been in Corsica when a local friend asked him to encourage more Britons to visit the island. Reitz looked into the numbers and worked out that he could charter a plane, book accommodation and sort out food cheaper together.

Love them or loathe them, package holidays – unlike their passengers – were here to stay.

DAYLIGHT SAVING TIME

Next time you're sipping a cool beer on a wonderful long summer evening, raise your glass to Victorian gent William Willett. He was out riding early one summer morning when he noticed how many blinds were still down, and the bright idea for daylight saving time came to him.

Electric lighting was extremely expensive, and Willett realised that gaining an extra hour of daylight when people were actually awake would save energy and money. He self-published *The Waste of Daylight* in 1907 but it wasn't until the First World War brought an urgent need to save coal that Britain finally introduced the scheme on this day 1916.

There is a sundial dedicated to Willett near his Kent home. It is set permanently to daylight saving time.

GEORGIE BEST

With his miraculous skill and superb goal-scoring, millions of football fans would certainly be happy to celebrate the life of George Best – who was born on this day in 1946. The fact that, off the field, he was a flawed man who lived his life to the full is also worth a cheer.

If only everyone was remembered by the following epitaph . . . 'I spent a lot of money on booze, birds and fast cars. The rest I just squandered.'

WORLD TURTLE DAY

Today's celebrations were started by American Tortoise Rescue in 2000 to help the world understand just how wonderful these reptiles are: they can swim at up to thirty five miles an hour, hold their breath for two hours, and have been around long enough to see the dinosaurs come and go.

Unfortunately, they also taste pretty good in soup, so today is also about discouraging people from eating them. So, try and refrain if you can . . .

THE KING OF THE JOKERS

Born today in 1879, Sorensen 'Sam' Adams was a man who liked to have fun. Specifically, he liked to laugh at other people . . . by playing jokes on them. I believe the official term is *schadenfreude*. Sam is probably responsible for inspiring more juvenile chuckles than any other japester in the world. Not only did he invent sneezing powder, but his company also created itching powder, the stink bomb, the hand buzzer, the fly-in-an-ice-cube and the dribble glass.

Funnily enough, Adams failed to see the funny side of the fart cushion, initially turning it down for being 'too vulgar'. Like a stink bomb is the height of sophistication . . .

STAR WARS DAY

It has made more people cheerful than almost any other film, but right up until this very day in 1977 – the day of the movie's release – the general opinion was quite the opposite. Distributors Twentieth Century Fox famously saw a rough cut and despaired. Lucas's own wife was in tears because she thought it was so awful. Only forty cinemas agreed to show it until the studio leaned on them. Lucas was close to a nervous breakdown. Then the film opened . . . and *something* happened . . . the queues went around the block. The blockbuster was born.

The movie changed the lives of millions of sci-fi geeks and the full Force of its influence can still be felt, such as the now-industry standard May release dates for 'event movies' to OTT merchandising.

MOUNT EVEREST DONE IN A DAY

While you're sitting on the loo reading this it might be cheering to note that on this day in 2003, a Sherpa called Lakpa Gelu quite simply got out of his chair at teatime to climb Mount Everest. He reached the top at 3.56a.m. the next morning – just ten hours and fifty six minutes after he set out. He was back in his tent for brunch by 11a.m. This, by the way, was only three days after he set the previous record for ascending Everest.

Oh, and it was the tenth time he had climbed the mountain.

So chin up, it's not too late to achieve something today!

THE FIRST WATERBED

If you've ever slept, relaxed or done anything else that's fun on a waterbed you'll know exactly why today needs to be celebrated.

Like the geostationary satellite (invented by Arthur C. Clarke in 1945), the waterbed was created by a science fiction writer – Robert Heinlein – who described one for the first time in his science fiction novel, *Stranger in a Strange Land*, published today in 1942.

NO FLY ZONE: MOSCOW'S RED SQUARE

Nineteen-year-old Mathias Rust dreamt of a better world during the Cold War in the 1980s. So he decided to illegally fly a plane into Moscow's Red Square. Thinking his flight would build an 'imaginary bridge' to the East, he rented a Cessna and told the flight tower he was heading to Stockholm. After he took off, he promptly turned the plane right. Jet fighters dispatched to intercept him lost contact, as did radar.

Rust, with his crazy plan still working, landed on a bridge near St Basil's cathedral, before taxiing into Red Square. He was arrested seconds later.

Rust was sentenced to four years in jail, but had the last laugh. His amateur flight through 'impregnable' Soviet air defences gave Mikhail Gorbachev the perfect excuse to fire dozens of military officials who were opposing him. This let him speed up his reforms, and bring the Cold War to an end earlier – Rust's flight of fancy, it seems, did actually make a difference.

THE POP-UP TOASTER

Is there any better pick-me-up than hot buttered toast? Inventor Charles Strite didn't think so when he filed the patent for the modern toaster on this very special day in 1919.

Toast, of course, had been around for quite some

time. But it always needed someone with a stick holding it against a flame or a grill that was hard to control. Strite set about inventing a toaster that didn't need constant tending. His breakthrough was combining springs and a variable timer – the same system used today.

EVEL KNIEVEL CRASHLANDS

Before he became a hero to millions of small boys in the 1970s, Evel Knievel was having a tough time standing out from other stunt riders.

Then he broke an arm and several ribs while failing to jump twelve cars and his crash brought him more publicity than the jump itself. People flocked to see him fly and tumble – and the bigger the crash, the bigger the cash. So when he successfully cleared sixteen cars on this day in 1967, it must have been something of a disappointment for the crowd – and Evel himself.

But he soon got his mojo back trying to jump the fountains at Caesar's Palace, Las Vegas. He ended up in a parking lot, breaking many bones and entering a twenty-nine-day coma.

His fame was assured.

READY, STEADY, ROLL!

Chasing cheese down a hill is great fun, at least according to the nutters who turn up at Cooper's Hill on this day every year.

The event begins when a circular Double Gloucester fromage is flung from Cooper's hilltop and competitors race down trying to catch it – usually tumbling and rolling themselves in the process. Since the cheese has a head start and can get up to seventy miles per hour, no one ever catches it. And that's it.

But like many quaint British traditions, the real point the day is to end up in a pub – the losers customarily console themselves with a ploughman's lunch at 'The Cheese Rollers' – so at least all that lunacy wasn't for nothing.

JUNE

CAKE CELEBRATION DAY

Today we celebrate cakes for the way they make us feel all cheerful inside. However, one cake above all others deserves special mention today – the Jaffa Cake.

Under UK law, no VAT is charged on biscuits and cakes. *Chocolate-covered* biscuits, however, must be taxed within an inch of their delicious lives. On this day in 1991 Customs and Excise called Jaffa's makers, McVities, into court claiming that Jaffa Cakes are, in fact, biscuits and therefore taxable. McVities pointed out that biscuits go soft when stale, but cakes go hard. Since Jaffa Cakes do the latter, they must be a cake. The judge agreed and VAT is not paid on Jaffa Cakes.

A glorious day for British justice.

MARCONI'S RADIO

Guglielmo Marconi probably had grander visions for his invention than a cacophony of loudmouth breakfast DJs, however, the invention of radio on this day 1896 is well worth celebrating.

Marconi was actually quite similar to many DJs in that he didn't really create anything new. His skill was in repackaging other people's material (rival inventor Nikola Tesla once claimed he was copying seventeen of his patents in a single device) and self-promotion. Marconi unified several existing technologies and then perfected the device, taking it from a gimmick that only worked over a few hundred yards to a transatlantic signalling service of global importance.

LAMB LIES DOWN WITH LIONS

Next time you feel like the world has thrown you to the lions, take heart at the story of the lamb that defied a king.

King James I wasn't one for animal welfare. He ordered trapdoors fitted into the Tower of London zoo so that dogs, bulls, bears and other poor creatures might be thrown to the lions for the entertainment of his court. And today in 1605, he took his family to see just such a spectacle. He had mutton dropped into the cages to get the lions' juices going, then the goodly king ordered a live lamb to be sent down. This quivering creature was lowered on a rope and fell helpless upon its knees. But rather than tear it apart, the giant cats simply stared at the lamb, and even when it tottered up close, they nuzzled it in loving sympathy.

James' bloodlust was thwarted, and the lamb was hauled up to safety. A gentle reminder that sometimes even the lions can be on your side.

HOLE IN THE WALL

Money from a wall? Sounds great, right? Well, that was finally made possible today in 1973 when Donald Wetzel, Tom Barnes and George Chastain patented the first-ever networked Automated Teller Machine (ATM).

Given that banks are useless, the ATM has proven itself to be a very useful invention.

However, ATMs are still prone to malfunction. In 2003, a couple went a little overboard when they discovered that a Coventry ATM was on the fritz – they promptly withdrew £134,410 in dozens of visits. They were tracked down rather easily and went straight to jail without passing go or collecting £200.

FIRST CLASS TRAVEL

A glamorous train journey with First Class service is guaranteed to speed your cares away – especially if you are one of the 750,000 stressed-out travellers who commute to London every day. And on this day in 1883, the still-one-of-a-kind Orient Express first puffed out of Paris, setting the standard for luxury rail travel. It also became internationally renowned for intrigue after Agatha Christie (the world's best-selling author of all time) plotted murder among its carriages in the kitchen-sink title *Murder on the Orient Express* in 1934.

SEX & THE CITY

For women, today's first US airing in 1998 of the critically acclaimed, popular (and controversial) TV show set fire to popular culture as we know it – spreading Girl Power all over the US. Set in the heart of Manhattan, *Sex & The City* was a window on a fabulous world of fashion, parties and female friendship and became a global phenomenon – proving that US dramas could be both adult and entertaining without sacrificing quality. Plus, it gave men an hour a week off to go and do what they wanted to do without wives or girlfriends caring where they were.

GANDHI'S NON-VIOLENT DISOBEDIENCE

Mohandas (not Mahatma) Gandhi was one of the world's most inspirational leaders and advocates of peace. He believed that all violence was evil and that the only way to oppose tyranny was non-cooperation, a positive philosophy that he first used on this day in 1893 in South Africa.

Gandhi's ideas and peaceful protests helped lead India to independence and inspired civil rights movements worldwide. Figures as diverse as Nelson Mandela, Martin Luther King, Barack Obama and John Lennon have all paid homage to his peaceful ways. If more people took a leaf out of Gandhi's book, the world would undoubtedly be a much more cheerful place.

THE BABY-JUMPING FESTIVAL OF CALACHO

Little towns all over the world have their own curious festivities. You can bet your life savings that somewhere in the world today, some town will be celebrating some crazy thing or another. A few of these are fun to join in with; others are simply there to make you glad you're not a local. This festival is one of the latter.

Held to celebrate the Catholic festival of Corpus Christi, this baby-jumping festival does what it says on the tin – grown men vaulting over newborn infants. Let me repeat that. *Grown men vaulting over newborn infants.* But there is also a rational reason behind this mad event – it's the best way to cleanse the babies of evil spirits. Of course.

THE ELECTRIC GUITAR IS BORN

You may not have heard of Lester Polfuss, but your favourite rock music simply wouldn't sound the same if he hadn't been born. Keith Richards, Paul McCartney, Eric Clapton, Peter Green, Jeff Beck, Jimmy Page, Billy Gibbons, Slash and many other legendary guitarists have all made their music on the guitar that bears his name.

Lester (aka Les Paul) was a brilliant guitarist and keen inventor. In 1940 he built a revolutionary instrument – the world's first solid-body Spanish guitar, known as 'The Log' because its core section was a lump of solid pine. He offered it to manufacturers Gibson but they weren't interested. Then the Fender Telecaster started an electric guitar craze and Gibson came scurrying back. Together they created the Gibson Les Paul, which became the preferred 'axe' of guitar heroes everywhere.

WONDERBRA

Whether you see it as a showcase of sexiness or deceptive subterfuge, the Wonderbra is undeniably brilliant. A survey in March 2008 of 3,000 UK women found that they considered the Wonderbra to be the greatest fashion innovation in history.

Thanks to the 'Hello Boys' commercials of the 1990s, it's easy to assume that the Wonderbra is a relatively recent product. But the name was first trademarked in the US in 1935, and the improved uplift design that we're familiar with was first patented today in 1941. At the peak of its popularity, a Wonderbra was sold every fifteen seconds in the US.

FERRIS BUELLER'S DAY OFF

Sometimes the only way you can cheer yourself up is by throwing a sickie, nicking a Ferrari and leading Chicago in a parade sing-a-long of 'Twist and Shout'. At least that was Ferris Bueller's idea in the iconic film that was released today in 1986.

The film lifted the hearts of all children growing up in the 1980s because Ferris was everything a teenager desperately wanted to be – rebellious, charming and cool. And for one glorious day Ferris sets about indulging in sheer happiness and freedom any and every way he can. Die hard fanatics of the film take the day off today too and just enjoy themselves in tribute to their screen hero.

THE INVENTION OF THE BICYCLE

It's weird to think that no one had ridden a bike before today in 1817, but that was the case when the bold Baron Karl von Drais first straddled his eponymous *draisine*. This was really a running machine, with a wooden frame supported by two in-line wheels. But it was a start, and soon other inventors had helped perfect the bike we know today.

If you haven't enjoyed the cheering powers of a bike ride recently, remember what Arthur Conan Doyle said: 'When the spirits are low, when the day appears dark, when work becomes monotonous, when hope hardly seems worth having, just mount a bicycle and go out for a spin down the road, without thought on anything but the ride you are taking'.

WORLD NETTLE-EATING CHAMPIONSHIPS

Regulars of the Bottle Inn in Marshwood, Dorset, decided to put together two things that usually live quite happily without one another – your mouth and nettles. And on this day they annually inaugurate the World Nettle-Eating Championships.

Nettles not only sting, but they also taste like 'a mixture of spinach and cow-pat'. You can't use any mouth-numbing substances, nor can you bring your own nettles (like you'd want to). And the sting in this tale? – it isn't even about how many nettles you can eat in a minute or something – the contest lasts for a whole *hour*.

GIVE US THIS DAY, OUR DAILY BOURBON

If you've ever enjoyed a cheeky Jack & Coke, today you ought to raise a cheer to Elijah Craig, who reputedly first distilled bourbon today in 1789.

Bourbon whiskey is made from at least fifty one per cent corn, rather than barley, which is used in Scotch whisky. It is then aged in charred-oak casks for four years, to impart its distinctive colour and taste. Almost all of it is made in Kentucky, which is where Elijah Craig built his pioneering distillery. Craig also built the county's first papermill – I guess because he needed labels for all those bottles.

When he wasn't starting a booze revolution, Elijah was a Baptist minister. Cheers, Reverend!

IN ROD WE TRUST

Flying a kite is one of life's great pleasures. Kites have also done their bit for science. Today in 1752, Benjamin Franklin famously used one to prove that lightning was an electrical phenomenon.

Of course, if Franklin had done as the legend states and actually flown his kite with a key attached into a full-blown storm, the only thing he would

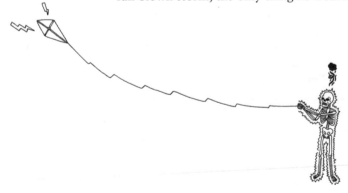

have proved was that electricity can kill you instantly. It's more likely that he flew the kite into clouds during the build-up of a storm, then brought it to earth to show it had been electrically charged. Franklin proved his point and used his knowledge to invent the lightning rod, which has since saved many a tall building from a heavenly electrical strike.

BLOOMSDAY

 Today in Dublin, fans of James Joyce take to the streets for Bloomsday, the celebration of this great writer. The day's fun is in reliving the events of Joyce's epic modernist novel *Ulysses*, which follows its hero Leopold Bloom through a single day – 16 June 1904.

To join the Bloomsdayers, you'll have to dress in Edwardian clothes and enjoy a breakfast of grilled mutton kidneys (in the book, these are described as having 'a faint tang of urine' – nice). You then embark on a cultural tour of Dublin – basically an all-day pub crawl.

However, the best thing about the day is that having soaked up all this knowledge about Ulysses, it saves you reading the book.

MARGHERITA'S PIZZA

In 1889, King Umberto I and Queen Margherita of Italy were visiting Naples. Word of a wonderful new concoction of flat bread, tomatoes and cheese had spread and the queen was keen to try it.

A visit by the royals to the peasant pizzeria that served the dish was out of the question. So word was sent to the owner Raffaele Esposito that Queen Margherita would like one of his signature dishes sent round – the first delivered pizza. In an intuitive bit of branding, Esposito used red tomato sauce, white mozzarella cheese and green basil leaves as toppings – the national colours of Italy.

The Queen loved the pizza, and the famous 'Margherita' was born. Esposito's Pizzeria still exists to this day.

WELLINGTON'S BOOT

The best thing about the Battle of Waterloo wasn't that the Duke of Wellington finally vanquished that rascal Napoleon . . . but that it immortalised the Wellington boot.

The standard military footwear of the time was the leather 'Hessian' boot (named after Hesse in Germany). But Wellington ordered from his shoemaker a custom-made version, cutting it to fit his leg more closely and using softer leather.

After his historic triumph at Waterloo today in 1815, the 'Wellington' became a must-have for every British gentleman who wished to show his cheerful patriotism.

JUNETEENTH

Juneteenth commemorates the freeing of the last US slaves in Texas in 1865. Also called Emancipation Day, it celebrates African-American heritage and the wider idea of freedom.

Although the importation of slaves had been banned years before, the fact that the children of slaves also became slaves meant that the big business of slave owning still rumbled on. Finally, today in 1865, the Thirteenth Amendment to the Constitution brought the good news that slavery itself was completely abolished.

Former slaves rejoiced in the streets, and this day has been recognised ever since.

INTERNATIONAL SURFING DAY

It's International Surfing Day today, which means every bodacious man and girl in the world who owns a surfboard will be cutting class and heading to the beach. Founded in 2004, at the height of summer solstice (when the waves are generally 'to the max'),

International Surfing Day aims to raise awareness for the environmental damage being done to the earth's oceans as well as encouraging people to cast off their nine-to-five shackles. Of course, if you live in Reading, this day tends to make more people miserable than cheery, but still . . .

MIDSUMMER

It's the longest day of the year (in non-leap years) and the traditional middle of summer, and it has brought cheer to societies around the world for thousands of years.

For pagans, midsummer was a night of magic and ritual that formed the most important festival of the year. This day was so important to many cultures that they constructed elaborate calendars to ensure they knew when it would fall, Stonehenge being the best example.

INTERNATIONAL GNOME DAY

International Gnome Day was started in 2002 to celebrate, if anything, our own eccentricity.

It's the biggest day of the year for those who enjoy a spot of gnome roaming (or 'gnoming'). This is the popular summer practice, undertaken by garden gnome liberationists, of stealing gnomes out of back gardens, taking photos of them in much more exotic climes, then sending the photos back to the owners. Some gnomes have made it as far away as Australia, upon which one relieved owner received a postcard from their gnome which read:

'Here I am at the Sydney Harbour Bridge. Having a wonderful holiday, love Gnorman'.

Fancy liberating a gnome? Today is the day.

THE PILL

Today in 1960, the Contraceptive Pill was born. Or more accurately, the FDA first approved it for use.

This tiny but incredibly powerful pill would mould a new economic role for women all over the world. Soon after it was legalised, college attendance and graduation rates for women shot up. Now that women could control their fertility, without sacrificing sexual relationships, they could make long-term educational and career plans. Within a few years the pill became immensely popular, playing a key role in the 1960s cultural revolution.

FIRST FLYING SAUCER

If it hadn't been for pilot Kenneth Arnold, there's a good chance that science fiction as we know it wouldn't exist. It was his sighting of UFOs flying near Mount Rainier, Washington, on this day in 1947 that seized the public imagination and led to the coining of the term 'flying saucer'.

Arnold saw a chain of eight disk-like and one crescent-shaped objects banking and darting in unison around the mountain. He worked out that they were flying at 1,700 miles per hour – three times faster than even the most advanced aircraft of the time.

Arnold's report fired UFOs and alien visitors into the public consciousness and inspired many out-of-this-world movies.

OUR WORLD BROADCAST

When you think of optimistic pop events that have cheered up the world, *Live Aid* immediately springs to mind. But the first live international satellite TV spectacular actually happened today in 1967.

Our World was a global gathering of top artists as diverse as Maria Callas and Pablo Picasso who performed live in the name of peace. The two-and-half-hour event pulled in 400 million viewers, the largest TV audience ever at that time. The UK's segment starred The Beatles, who performed their new song, 'All You Need Is Love'. With the Vietnam war raging, the song's powerful message and OTT performance created one of the most captivating and celebratory moments caught on telly.

RATCATCHERS DAY

It was on this day in 1284 that the Pied Piper allegedly spirited away the children of Hamlin, Germany, after the town's residents refused to pay him for curing their rat infestation.

Although the Pied Piper's story may sound like a myth there is actually an undercurrent of truth to the tale with many references to the incident reported in the official annals of the town.

Anyway, the cheering moral of today is that if a man in

patterned pyjamas wanders into your town and successfully entices all the rodents away *by playing the piccolo*, you might want to pay the bill.

HAPPY BIRTHDAY MILDRED HILL

'Happy Birthday To You' was written by teacher Mildred Hill in 1859, whose birthday it is today. She and her sister Patty composed 'Good Morning To All', as a song that children could easily learn. This gradually morphed into 'Happy Birthday To You' – same tune, different lyrics.

The copyright of the song is owned by Warner Chappell and they insist on collecting a royalty every time it is performed in public. In 2008, they earned $2 million. In theory, if you sing it at a party where a lot of the guests aren't friends or family, you should pay them a royalty . . . but the fact that you never will should be a very cheering thought.

SKIING ON WATER

Occasionally someone has an idea that is obviously insane, but by sticking at it, they go on to show the world that they weren't so bonkers after all.

Take Ralph Samuelson. Today in the summer of 1922 he was just an eighteen-year-old boy who thought it would be great if you could ski on water like you could on snow. So he strapped barrel staves onto his feet and tied himself to a powerboat. He fell over. He then tried normal snow skis, but they too failed to function on water. Finally he got some pine planks that were eight feet long and nearly a foot wide and bent the ends up by boiling them in his mother's kettle.

He must have looked ridiculous. Nonetheless, on this day a new sport was born.

NO BUSINESS LIKE SNOW BUSINESS

Snowmobiles aren't just a cool way to get about in the cold, they're essential if you're going to have a ski-chase scene in an action film. And they only exist thanks to Joseph-Armand Bombardier who patented his snowmobile caterpillar-track system today in 1937.

People had been sticking skis on cars for years, but the tricky winter conditions in Canada meant that horse-drawn sleighs were the only real way of getting about for large parts of the year. Not good if you needed a doctor. Then Bombardier got busy inventing and cracked his traction system which propelled snowmobiles carrying up to twelve people. Once smaller engines came on the scene, Bombardier also invented the one-man machine known as the 'Ski-doo'.

HULA HOOP

Richard Knerr may not be a household name but on this day in 1958 his company launched the Hula Hoop and in one fell swoop cheered up bored children everywhere.

His creation became a worldwide sensation, selling 100 million within a year. Of course, as with any fad, sales dropped off pretty quickly. But Mr Knerr was no one-trick pony, and he got the company ready to produce another toy idea he had up his sleeve which no one else believed in, a flying plastic disc called the Frisbee. It took off, apparently.

JULY

WALK THIS WAY

 Today in 1979, Sony launched the Walkman – the first personal entertainment device. One person less than delighted at the appearance of this new technology, however, was Andreas Pavel. He had long dreamt of 'adding a soundtrack to real life', and in 1972 had invented the 'Stereobelt', a portable cassette player with headphones. He had shown it to all the major electronics manufacturers, and they laughed in his face – no one would be daft enough to wear headphones in public, they said. Nevertheless, Pavel knew he was onto a winner and had several patents pending when Sony launched their (suspiciously) similar device.

Pavel sued and received a cash payment rumoured to be over $10,000,000 and royalties on future Walkman models. Must have been music to his ears.

WIFE-CARRYING CHAMPIONSHIP

This crazy annual competition started today in the town of Sonkajärvi, Finland, in 1994 as an amusing way of commemorating the ancient 'practice' of stealing women from neighbouring villages. The poor, poor man has to carry his wife over a 253.5 metre-long obstacle track complete with water hazard and log hurdles.

You might think the wives have it easy, but in the popular 'Estonian' carrying position, the wife's face is usually plumb in her beloved one's bottom, so it's not like it's all fun and games.

STRAWBERRIES

Strawberries have been a particularly cheerful fruit ever since Mickey Rourke fed them to a blindfolded Kim Basinger in the steamy *9½ Weeks*. But that scene wouldn't have been half as much fun if it hadn't been for a humble market gardener from Isleworth called Michael Keens.

For centuries, strawberries could only be picked in the wild, making them rare and troublesome. But Mr Keens saw the potential and dedicated years to cultivating the seductive strawb, and today in 1806 he exhibited the first-ever successful cultivar. Like all modern strawberries, the variety that Ms Basinger enjoyed *so* much are descended from his 'Keens' Seedling'.

ADVENTURES IN WONDERLAND

If it hadn't been for a simple boat ride taken today in 1862, the world would be without one of its most beloved and influential books.

Lewis Carroll (mathematician Charles Lutwidge Dodgson, actually) was idling along the Thames with a friend and three children. To keep the youngsters amused, he spun them a yarn, apparently off the top of his head, about a girl called Alice who follows a white rabbit down a hole. There she discovers a wonderful world of weird characters, warped logic and nonsense verse.

Queen Victoria loved the book so much that she requested Carroll dedicate his next publication to her. She was duly presented with a mathematical work with the less than wonderful title, *An Elementary Treatise on Determinants*.

THE BIKINI

If it wasn't for French designer Louis Reard, women might still be going swimming in several square yards of taffeta.

But brave Louis took a large pair of scissors to the traditional swimsuit and created a daring two-piece design. He knew it looked stunning, but finding a model to wear such a scandalous creation was an issue. Eventually he turned to 'exotic dancer' Micheline Bernardini, who on this day in 1946 unveiled Louis' bikini to a literally blown-away world.

Indeed, Reard called it the 'bikini' because the US atomic test explosion at Bikini Atoll in the Pacific Ocean had happened the same week.

RUNNING OF THE BULLS

Ever since Ernest Hemingway wrote adoringly about it in *The Sun Also Rises*, the bull run in Pamplona has become the daftest thing in the world to do.

The run itself (or *encierro*) is part of the eight-day festival of San Fermín, and it started as a way of getting the animals from the corral where they slept to the bullring. As the bulls were shooed through the streets, citizens would leap in front of them to show their bravery. Now it's mostly cocky young tourists who have a go. The sight of silly buggers being trampled by one of nature's powerhouses shouldn't cheer you up, but it does.

THE GREATEST THING SINCE ITSELF

If you've ever butchered a loaf of bread trying to cut your own slices, you'll appreciate that this day in 1928 saw pre-sliced bread sold for the first time.

The commercial 'automatic bread-slicing machine' was built by US inventor Otto Frederick Rohwedder. His first attempt at such a machine ominously caught fire but, undeterred, the next attempt was a cut above the rest and was soon slicing bread the world over. The marketing slogan for his new product was 'the greatest forward step in the baking industry since bread was wrapped', so actually, it seems, the greatest thing before sliced bread was just wrapped bread.

ROSWELL

The first furore surrounding our modern obsession with extraterrestrial hullabaloo started on this day in 1947 when the local air base in Roswell, New Mexico, issued a press statement reporting it had found a crashed 'flying disk'. After an initial media flurry, the incident was virtually forgotten until 1978 when a UFO researcher reignited interest. This was coincidentally a year after the film *Close Encounters of the Third Kind* was released.

Whether a spacecraft crashed or not, the once-dull industrial town is now a tourist hot-spot and ground zero for alien conspiracies.

MEGA-TSUNAMI CONFIRMED

Geologists had long theorised that a major rockfall could generate a mega-tsunami, or giant wave of hitherto unseen dimensions. But this remained a hypothesis until an earthquake on this day in 1958 caused ninety million tons of rock to sheer off a mountain in Lituya Bay, Alaska. The block fell vertically and hit the water with cataclysmic force, causing a wave an incredible 1,724 feet high to surge down the fjord-like bay.

Two people who were probably less than delighted at the sight of this science in action were Howard Ulrich and his son Edrie.

They were in a boat in the same bay, fishing, as the wave higher than *any skyscraper on Earth* came roaring towards them. Astonishingly they survived, their boat safely surfing the biggest wave ever recorded.

LADY GODIVA RIDES OUT

When you're being hammered by unfair taxes, there isn't much that can raise your spirits. But a beautiful duchess riding naked down the high street might just do the trick.

Lady Godiva was an eleventh-century noblewoman whose husband, Leofric, had been frittering public cash while local people lived in poverty. He proposed a poll tax to cover his spending. His outraged wife demanded he lift the tax, or at least use the money to provide art for the benefit of the peasants. Leofric agreed on one condition – that she ride naked on horseback through the town.

So, at noon on this day in the year 1040, Lady Godiva gave the citizens of Coventry a rather different sort of public art to enjoy. And the taxes, like her clothing, were removed.

CULTURED PEARLS

If you're a glamour girl (or plan on buying a nice present for one), today you can thank Japanese entrepreneur Mikimoto Kōkichi for bringing perfect pearls within the price range of mere mortals.

Before Mikimoto created the first cultured pearls on this day in 1893, it was natural pearls or nothing. Since these were rare beyond belief they were also fiercely expensive. So Mikimoto mastered the method of producing round pearls of exceptional quality to order – for a fraction of the cost of 'natural' jewels. More than ninety nine per cent of all pearls sold today are cultured.

Mikimoto's technique involves grafting tissue from a donor oyster into the gonad of another mollusc. So, in a way, cultured pearls are literally the oyster's balls.

ROLLING STONES START ROCKING

If you're partial to a spot of the Rolling Stones then today in 1962 gave you a lot to be cheerful about. It was their first gig.

One man who was particularly delighted to see this exciting new group was the talent scout man at Decca Records, Dick Rowe. He had previously made the rather large error of rejecting The Beatles with the famous pronouncement, 'Guitar groups are on their way out, Mr Epstein'.

It was such a blunder that even The Beatles felt sorry for him – Rowe was told about the Rolling Stones by George Harrison. He wasn't going to make the same mistake twice and signed Mick & co instantly, which must go down as one of history's all-time great saves.

BOB GELDOF'S NUMBERS

As the world's biggest fund-raising concert, *Live Aid* proved it was possible to make life better for people who had suffered in a terrible humanitarian disaster – the Ethiopian famine. Today in 1985 nearly 200,000 rock fans in two stadia and 400 million viewers tuned in to do their bit.

However, this day goes down in TV infamy as the day Bob Geldof cheered up the whole country by telling a BBC presenter to 'Fuck the address, let's get the numbers!' (Not as people think they remember: 'Give us your fucking money'). The phones went red hot and donations shot up to £300 per second. The final figure raised by *Live Aid* was £150 million.

BASTILLE DAY

Today we have a big reason to be cheerful as it commemorates the toppling of one of history's most notorious monarchies and the establishment of important social ideals of liberty and equality.

The storming of the Bastille was the tipping point in France's long-bubbling social uprising as the Bastille was a hated symbol of absolute royal power. Not that the storming itself was done to free hordes of falsely imprisoned, innocent citizens – the Bastille only held seven inmates at the time. The cheeky revolutionaries were in fact after the 30,000 pounds of gunpowder stored inside. Still, Revolutionaries 1, Royalty 0.

THE PLATYPUS FIRST SWIMS INTO THE PUBLIC EYE

It has a muzzle like a duck's bill and a beaver's tail, it lays eggs and *also* suckles its young – the platypus is living proof that God enjoys the odd cheerful day, too.

It's no wonder that the Europeans who saw the first platypus pelts sent back from Australia thought they were the work of a taxidermist with a weird sense of humour and a Frankenstein complex. And its habits were as tricky to understand as its appearance: the creature was almost impossible to rear in captivity. It wasn't until this day in 1922 that the first public appearance (outside Australia) of the Platypus was unveiled at New York Zoo.

ALIENS RECOGNISED BY LAW

Want proof that aliens are out there? Well, you can take cheer from the fact that today in 1969 (just a few days before the first moon landing) the US actually passed a law enshrining extraterrestrials on the statute books.

The law is real enough, although it's buried in the 1,211th subsection of the fourteenth section of a bunch of regulations that have hardly even been read by many members of the government. The bad news is that the law made contact between US citizens and extraterrestrials strictly illegal, under threat of a year in jail and a $5,000 fine.

Which sounds bad, until you realise that if there weren't something out there, why would they bother with such a law . . . ?

AIR ... ON ONE CONDITION

Today we raise a chilled-out cheer to modern air conditioning, one of life's loveliest luxuries ... if you live somewhere hot that is.

Invented by Willis Carrier today in 1902, the first modern air-conditioning unit was designed to help a printing company run their presses more efficiently. Mr Carrier simply took the concept of steam heating and reversed the process. Rather than sending air through hot coils, he used coils filled with cold water. This cooled the air and also allowed him to control the level of moisture in the atmosphere.

Great news for the hot and bothered everywhere.

ELVIS INVENTED

There are millions of truck drivers, but there's only ever been one Elvis. So we should all be glad that today in 1953, the eighteen-year-old truck driver decided to record a song for his mother.

When he walked in off the dusty Memphis streets to Sun Record Studios and sang 'My Happiness' he was, unbeknownst to him, about to invent modern rock 'n' roll. His recordings caught the ear of studio boss Sam Phillips who called Presley back for an audition. Presley started this by singing country and western standards but, sensing he was blowing it, kicked into a blistering version of 'That's All Right'. Phillips was wowed and a week later the song was in the charts.

The world had one less truck driver and one more King.

BEACH VOLLEYBALL

Today in 1996 the Atlanta Olympics opened, and beach volleyball hit millions of screens for the first time. For many, the sight of swimsuit-clad, super-athletic, bronzed bodies of both sexes sweating hard in the sun was more like a show than a sport. For viewers bored of rowing and shot-putting it suddenly made the Olympics worth watching again.

SPECIAL OLYMPICS FOUNDED

The Special Olympics started on this day in 1968 in Chicago. PE teacher Anne Burke only planned the event as a one-off, but the idea soon spread on an international scale. Today the movement gives empowerment to more than three million athletes and inspires change in 170 countries.

In fact, at the 1999 Special Olympics World Games, Israeli and Palestinian athletes competed side-by-side in the doubles table-tennis competition. While in Iraq and Afghanistan, Special Olympics athletes have been seen practicing in the lulls between bombings. And despite their problems, both countries sent delegations to compete in the 2003 and 2007 World Summer Games.

Give these winners a cheer . . .

MEN ON THE MOON

Men. On the moon. Today in 1969. That is still massively impressive.

It had only been eight years since JFK had seriously launched the idea into motion – NASA hadn't even sent a man into orbit by then. It required an astonishing burst of creativity and technical progress before the impossible dream became real.

For perspective, the Satellite Navigation GSP in your car might have a memory of two gigabytes. The guidance computer that navigated the astronauts to earth's actual satellite *240,000 miles away* had just two kilobytes. So your SatNav is a million times more powerful than a spaceship *that flew to the moon*, and it still has trouble getting you to Windermere.

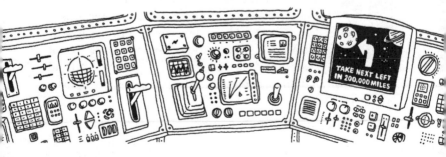

PI DAY

Today we celebrate a vital mathematical constant. Pi is an irrational number approximating 3.14, or as an approximate fraction, 22/7. It is important because . . . well, it just is.

Archimedes started Pi Day back in ancient Greece when he approximated the number as being 22/7, which is also the notation for 22 July. Today, mathematicians the world over will celebrate by holding Pi-reciting competitions – the current record is a ridiculous 83,431 places.

A REALLY COOL INVENTION

It was on this day in 1904 that Charles Menches first gave people the chance to savour their creamed ice in a wonderful, edible cone.

Milk and fruit ices had been around for centuries – Marco Polo was said to have brought a particularly delicious recipe back from China. Ice cream has been mass-produced since 1851 and people often ate it from paper or metal cones. But Menches' genius idea (upon running out of plates one day) was to make a cone from a rolled-up waffle (sold on a nearby stand) that people could also eat, and in doing so he invented the sweetest pick-me-up ever.

MACHU PICCHU

When US historian Hiram Bingham pushed back the jungle creepers on this day in 1911 to reveal Machu Picchu, his eyes must have popped out of his head. He had rediscovered the 'Lost City of the Incas', forgotten for centuries, and a cultural and architectural masterpiece.

Machu Picchu is in a truly remarkable location – it perches on a mist-shrouded mountain-top with vertical cliffs on three sides dropping 1,500 feet to a pounding river. And it was thanks to this precipitous position that the ancient city's architecture remained intact for so long. Once the jungle was cleared, a remarkable, unbelievable collection of houses, temples and terracing appeared exactly as they had been left 500 years earlier.

FIRST TEST TUBE BABY BORN

When Louise Brown popped into the world today in 1978, it was obviously a joyous day for her parents who had been unsuccessfully trying for children for nine years. It also opened a door of happiness for millions of families all over the world.

In vitro fertilisation (IVF) is the proper name for the procedure in which egg cells are fertilised outside, rather than inside, the womb. And the fertilisation is actually usually done in a Petri dish, not a test-tube. It's a process that doctors have got better and better at, and an incredible three million people in the UK wouldn't be here if it weren't for IVF, with 200,000 more bouncing babies joining us every year.

THE BEANO

In our age of iPods and Facebook, it's great to think that *The Beano* is still making children chuckle. It's been stashed inside schoolbooks for generations, and it first appeared on this day way back in 1938.

Kids loved *Beano* characters like the rebellious Dennis the Menace, but the comic was often criticised for encouraging bad behaviour. However, it is now officially the world's longest running weekly comic.

Another memorable Beano Day was 2 August 2008 – Gnashional Menace Day – when children were sponsored to behave like Dennis. This event raised many thousands of pounds for charity. How much was spent tidying up the chaos they caused was not reported.

NATIONAL SLEEPY HEAD DAY

The Finns are clearly a fun-loving bunch of people, what with the Wife-Carrying Championships (2 July) and today – National Sleepy Head Day.

This isn't some promotional marketing nonsense from a gift-card corporation, but an ancient tradition based on the fabled Saints of Ephesus who slumbered in a cave for over 200 years back in the Middle Ages. The idea is simple: whoever is last out of bed in the house gets a bucket of water thrown over them. Better set your alarm . . .

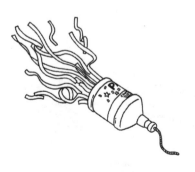

LAWN MOWER ENDURANCE RACE

Just because you can't afford a fancy sports car, doesn't mean you can't enjoy the thrills of motorsport. All you need is a lawnmower.

The 12-hour Endurance Race is the highlight of The British Lawn Mower Racing Association's event calendar and is held today. Like all BLMRA races, it's strictly old-school amateur – you can't soup-up your mower's engine and no sponsorship is allowed. As soon as you join the Association you'll be eligible to enter, but you'd better be prepared for some stiff competition – previous winners include Sir Stirling Moss and Derek Bell.

Some lawn mowers (not mine) average over 23mph, so in the twelve hours you could actually cover over 300 miles.

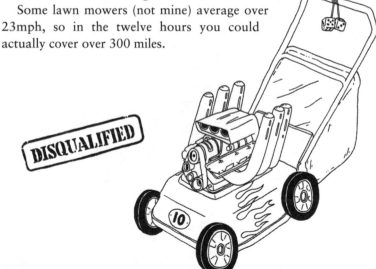

FIESTA OF NEAR-DEATH EXPERIENCES

Being hit by a truck is something you might want to forget about. But coming close to death is actually being proudly celebrated today in Las Nieves in Spain.

The day might seem a little less than cheery at first – the near-deathers start by going to church in a coffin.

But this day isn't just about confronting the dark reality of death. It's also a reminder of all the wonderful things that the near-deathers have come back to. With the solemnities over, the tone changes to one of jubilation. Fireworks fill the sky, brass bands belt out the tunes, fine food and drink flow freely, and the streets fill with people sharing their joy at being alive.

ENGLAND WIN THE WORLD CUP

On this day in 1966 England's football team won the World Cup. It was a jolly cheerful day to be English.

For the final, 93,000 spectators – including the Queen and Prince Phillip – packed Wembley Stadium to see England beat Germany 4-2 in extra time thanks to Geoff Hurst's stunning hat-trick (which remains, stat-fans, the only one ever scored in a World Cup final).

As the match was in its last seconds, some delirious fans ran onto the grass. 'Some people are on the pitch,' commentator

Kenneth Wolstenholme related very, very excitedly '. . . they think it's all over . . . it is now!' Sadly, this has never been repeated.

BONJOUR, BRITISH BANGERS

Three years is a distressingly long time to go without a great British banger on your barbecue (unless you're vegetarian, of course). So it was great news for continental sausage lovers when the European Commission finally cleared British beef for export today in 1999.

It had been off the menu following the BSE 'mad cow' crisis – after all, no one wanted their bangers to send them bonkers. But stricter hygiene standards now meant that British beef was the best around, so steak fans could tuck in with relish. Or mustard. And onions, don't forget the onions.

AUGUST

FIRST SCOUT CAMP

 If you were one of the millions of boys around the world who went on a Scout Camp and learned survival skills, lifesaving and wondering what on earth a woggle is for, then today's the day to find your little hat from the loft and throw it in the air and cheer for the first ever Scout camp.

Boer War hero Robert Baden-Powell was fascinated by the skills of African military scouts, and wrote a book about their techniques. To test this out, he gathered a group of lads and headed off to Brownsea Island on this day in 1907. His venture was a huge success and his book *Scouting for Boys* in 1908 became the fourth best-selling title of all time.

KNACKERED?

If you live in a crazy hick town where there is nothing to do, why don't you take a leaf out of the books of the good people of Clinton, Montana, who today celebrate their nuts at their annual Testicle Festival.

You might think that testicles aren't the most spectacular of things to celebrate but the locals have been plum crazy since 1982. They will chomp their way through fifty four tons of Rocky Mountain Oysters – deep fried bull balls, in case you didn't know. Those spectators in need of a break from all this nutty nonsense can enjoy a Body Painting Contest, the Naked Pool Tournament or even Bullshit Bingo, in which you bet on when a bull will take a dump.

Highbrow it isn't, but you're guaranteed to have a ball.

COLUMBUS AND THE NEW WORLD

If you're feeling like you can't be arsed to do anything today then you should take your motivational inspiration from Christopher Columbus who set sail on his first famous voyage of discovery on this day in 1492.

Columbus was aiming to find a westerly route to the Orient, which he had calculated to be only 3,000 miles away. He was wrong. It is 12,000 miles away, and Columbus and his crew would certainly have starved to death had he not had the sheer good fortune to bump into a totally unknown continent just when they were running out of biscuits.

CHAMPAGNE AND THE MONK

'Come quickly, I am drinking the stars!' cried Dom Perignon supposedly on this day in 1693. And no wonder he was so happy – he'd just invented champagne.

Even better is the fact that Dom wasn't a vineyard owner or businessman, but a Benedictine monk. Exactly what a monk was doing producing the world's favourite party drink, we're not sure, but we're very, very happy that he did. Mind you, what with all those Belgian monasteries and their Trappist beers, and the Buckfast-producing friars of Devon, it's clear that being a monk isn't about a quiet life of piety, it's about getting quietly pie-eyed.

INTERNATIONAL BEER DAY

There are plenty of celebrations where beer is the key ingredient to fun times, but none of them were solely about beer itself – until the first International Beer Day righted that heinous wrong in 2007.

By putting beer at the centre of the fun, you don't have any of the time-wasting stuff of other celebrations

– like pretending to honour St Patrick or travelling to Germany for Oktoberfest. International Beer Day leaves more time to dedicate to beer and your friends and hopefully it will become a national holiday soon – all it needs is your ale-hearted support.

HARRY HOUDINI'S FEAT

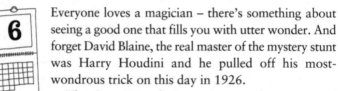

Everyone loves a magician – there's something about seeing a good one that fills you with utter wonder. And forget David Blaine, the real master of the mystery stunt was Harry Houdini and he pulled off his most-wondrous trick on this day in 1926.

The Great Houdini was immensely strong and flexible, highly skilled and he had a knack for showmanship – he used to escape from straitjackets by dislocating his own shoulders. And today he spent an hour in a straitjacket, in a sealed coffin at the bottom of a swimming pool before escaping.

Did he do it by slowing down his metabolism? Did he put himself in a coma? I have no idea . . . but trying to work it out is half the fun.

MAN ON WIRE

Occasionally someone does something so audacious that it takes your breath away just thinking about it. Like on this day in 1974, when wire-walker Philip Petit stepped off the roof of the South Tower of the World Trade Centre, New York, and into the history books.

Petit spent six years planning what he called the 'artistic crime of the century' – walking from tower to tower on a wire, a quarter of a mile above the Manhattan sidewalks. When he finally got up there, Petit crossed the void *eight times* and even performed a few tricks, sitting down on the wire, saluting with his knees and even lying on his back to chat to an inquisitive seagull.

PIG OUT AT LA POURCAILHADE

If you've ever been out-cooled by a French person, you'll find it cheering to know that for today at least they'll be making themselves look *très* silly at the annual Festival of the Pig in Trie Sur Baïse.

The pick of the porky madness is the prestigious *Cri du Cochon*, a pig impersonation contest. Don't think you can just turn up and start oinking, though. You must impersonate a specific episode in a porcine life, perhaps the squeals of a suckling piglet, or the grunts of a porker rolling in mud. This being France there's also quite a lot of pig eating to be done too. In fact, the festival once created the world's longest sausage – over one third of a mile long.

BIRDS, BEES, BEN & JERRY'S

Vanilla is now one of the world's best-loved flavourings. But it's only thanks to a slave boy messing around with a few blades of grass today in 1841 that you can even enjoy it at all.

Before this day, the coquettish vanilla orchid refused to be pollinated by any bee other than the local bees in its native Mexico. This made it impossible to produce the very tasty vanilla beans profitably. Then twelve-year-old slave Edmond Albius hand-pollinated an orchid with a wiggle of a blade of grass and a dab of his thumb. It was now profitable to grow vanilla beans without bees.

Today, the majority of the world's vanilla is made in Madagascar where every flower is still individually pollinated with Edmond's technique.

HOTTEST DAY EVER

The British climate often gets in the way of being cheerful – usually it's too cold, too wet, too windy or too much of all three. But today in 1983, not even the grumpiest man alive could complain.

It was roasting everywhere, the mercury reaching a skin-sizzling 38.5°C (101.3°F) in Kent – the first time 100 degrees Fahrenheit had been reached in the UK since records began.

NATIONAL SMILE WEEK

With smiling banned from UK passports because the scanners can't cope with them, it's good news for us cheerful types that National Smile Week starts today.

There are over fifty types of smile, the sincerest of all being the *Duchenne* smile – the one that pushes up into your eyes. It's more genuine apparently because when you're really happy, you use involuntary muscles to express your pleasure. That's why fake smiles stand out a mile and lead to distrust – Tony Blair's famous grin being a prime ministerial example.

PERSEID METEOR SHOWER

Shooting stars have entranced humans for millennia, and although they normally appear fleetingly throughout the year, tonight's show is guaranteed.

That's because the Earth is passing through a cloud of dust ejected by the tail of comet Swift-Tuttle. These particles smash into earth's atmosphere at high speed and burn up, causing the cosmic light show. You can see the Perseid shower from mid-July each year, but the peak is tonight (well, early this morning) when you could catch more than sixty an hour.

LEFT-HANDERS' DAY

If anyone deserves a bit of fun today, it's lefties. History has often been cruel to left-handers – the word 'sinister' comes from the Latin for 'left-handed'. And manufacturers of can openers, corkscrews and scissors rarely consider their southpaw sensibilities. Which is hardly fair considering how much lefties contribute to society – five out of the last seven US presidents have been left-handers.

Lefties, however, aren't allowed to play polo using their favoured hand. Which seems a bit unfair since most horses are left-footed and they're allowed to play.

FIRST BEAUTY PAGEANT

For some women it's a showcase for all that's beautiful about femininity. For others, it's a sexist parade that demeans women. But there certainly are a lot of people who enjoy looking at beautiful ladies, and they've seen a lot of entertainment over the years thanks to the pioneering contest started today in 1908.

The boss of Folkestone pier came up with the idea as a way to draw in more visitors. Even 100 years ago, his idea was a bit controversial, with suffragettes packing out the first two rows to protest. But the crowd – and the girls themselves – loved it, and the event was hugely popular. It went on to inspire even grander pageants such as Miss World.

THE FUN STARTS HERE

What do you love most about amusement parks – the exciting rides, the beautiful gardens, the laughing children, the hour-long queues for a £10 hot dog? Well, none of it would exist if it weren't for the Tivoli Gardens in Copenhagen, which opened today in 1843.

Tivoli's founder was granted the land for the park because he told the Danish king that 'when the people are amusing themselves, they do not think about politics'.

Walt Disney upon visiting Tivoli Gardens was so impressed

with its 'happy and unbuttoned air of relaxed fun' that he set out to shape Disneyland in its image.

IL PALIO, SIENA

Back in 1656 the locals of a quiet Tuscan town once asked 'how can we make our annual horse race more exciting?' To which some bright spark answered 'Let's hold it in the cobbled town square and ban saddles'.

'Il Palio' is still run to this day, and it really is cool. One moment you're sitting in a café, sipping sangiovese and nibbling gnocchi, the next the world's most thrilling horse race is thundering past your table.

LEWDNESS WITH LEWINSKY

After months of vigorous denial, today was the day Bill Clinton finally – ahem – came clean and admitted to an inappropriate relationship with White House intern Monica Lewinsky.

For comedy value this story is hard to beat. The most powerful man on the planet was accused of being caught pants down with a junior staffer. He strenuously denied it, but it was blindingly obvious to everyone that he was fibbing – the stories of the stained dress and the cigar tube were simply too good to have been made up.

Clinton was eventually acquitted of his impeachment charges, presumably because everyone had had such a laugh for so long at his expense.

JIMI HENDRIX'S WOODSTOCK

Today, in 1969, Jimi Hendrix's Woodstock performance changed the face of rock 'n' roll. His two-hour set featured Hendrix classics including 'Foxy Lady', 'Voodoo Child' and 'Hey Joe', but it was his feedback-drenched version of the 'Star-Spangled Banner' that suddenly gave the rising disillusionment of the American Dream an anthem.

PHOTOGRAPHY GIVEN TO THE WORLD

Photos are a fun part of our modern lives that we pretty much take for granted. But until this day in 1839, having an image of yourself was a luxury reserved for those who could afford to pay an artist to sit and paint them – only the wealthy, in other words.

Then Louis-Jacques Daguerre invented the first large-scale successful photographic technique, the Daguerreotype. The French Government bought his patent and in an extraordinary show of generosity, today in 1839 announced that the invention was a gift 'Free to the World'. For the first time ever, people could get an exact likeness of themselves and their family at a reasonable price, and the Daguerrotype was a monumental hit.

IN MEMORY OF HUNTER S. THOMPSON

 When hard-drinking, drug-scoffing, gun-loving, authority-baiting gonzo journo Hunter S. Thompson checked himself out, his family and friends wanted to find a suitable way to remember him. Luckily Hunter already had a plan in place and on this day in 2005 his vision was gloriously put into action.

Erected near his home in Colorado after his death, Hunter's creation was a 153 foot tower (two feet taller than the Statue of Liberty) in the shape of a two-thumbed fist clutching a peyote button. With a cannon on top. Loaded with fireworks packed with Hunter's ashes. His remains were then blasted into red, white, blue and green stars beside a full moon.

EXTREME POGOPALOOZA

Today's reason to be cheerful is Pogopalooza – the tongue-twisting festival of Extreme Pogo that is held on this day every year. The pogo stick was invented in 1914, but it was when Extreme Pogo sticks were created that the sport really took off – literally. These mechanical monsters now use hydraulics to supercharge their jumping ability. This means pogo-ers can now do amazing tricks, flips, twists and jumps over eight feet – much, much more than conventional pogos. If you have still got your stick from when you were a kid, soup up with a piston or two, and then head to your local A&E.

THE INVENTION OF THE DISHWASHER

If you hate washing up (and who doesn't) today you should be very happy that Mrs Josephine Cochrane shared your dish-pleasure.

Mrs Cochrane was a nineteenth century American socialite whose careless servants one day chipped her family china. Unacceptable. But since she didn't want to wash her own dishes, the only solution was to invent a machine that would do the job. So Josephine took herself off to her library and half an hour later came up with the idea of using pressurised water as a cleaning mechanism, sprayed onto dishes held fast on a rack – a design that hasn't changed.

Josephine's invention was demonstrated for the first time on this day in 1893 at the World's Fair, where apparently it cleaned up.

CROP CIRCLES

Occasionally drinking with your mates in a pub gives birth to some fantastic ideas. Like the one Doug Bower and his pal Dave Chorley had today in 1976.

The pranksters were drinking in a Hampshire pub one night when they thought of the type of patterns that would occur *if* a UFO were to land on Earth. Using wooden planks and rope, Doug and Dave created ever more intricate and beautiful designs for years to follow.

But the world would never have known the hoaxers' identities if it hadn't been for Bower's wife accusing him of adultery. She'd clocked the high mileage in their car and got suspicious. Forced to 'fess up his mischief, he thought he might as well tell the papers the whole corny story too.

A NEW TWIST ON AN OLD IDEA

Bits of cork in wine always piss people off. Reverend Samuel Henshall agreed and today in 1795 patented the first modern corkscrew.

The good vicar's big idea was to have a 'button' between the screw and the shank that stopped the worm going too far into the cork. It also compressed and turned the cork, unsticking it from the neck of the bottle.

Henshall's design is still in use – over 200 years and millions of bottles later.

FIRST CARNEGIE LIBRARY

'The man who dies rich, dies disgraced,' thought 19th century industrialist Andrew Carnegie, so on this day in 1883 he opened the first of his free public libraries in his hometown of Dunfermline.

Carnegie would go on to fund, build and stock an incredible 2,500 public libraries across the UK and US. Carnegie was also the first to allow readers to browse books and choose their own titles without asking a clerk. This had a fabulous knock-on effect on the education and freedom of knowledge for future generations.

Carnegie's fortune, in today's terms, would be valued at $300 billion. Bill Gates is currently worth 'just' $40 billion.

SLIPPERS

Slippers are brilliant. Slipping on a pair will cheer you up instantly no matter how miserable your day has been. And for this privilege we must thank Prince Albert, who slipped into being today in 1819.

The king of slipper designs is still called the Prince Albert. This velvet slipper has a plain leather sole and quilted silk lining in a contrasting colour. They really are very fine indeed. So, wrench off your boots and go slip into something more comfortable . . . and relax.

THE GUINNESS BOOK OF RECORDS

If you've ever had an argument you couldn't settle, be grateful today for the publication of the first-ever *Guinness Book of Records* in 1955.

It, too, started with an argument. Sir Hugh Beaver, the managing director of Guinness Breweries was debating with a shooting chum about which game bird flew away from their guns the fastest. No reference book could supply their answer so Sir Hugh recruited the brainiac McWhirter twins and together they produced the first *Guinness Book of Records*. Intended just to be a marketing ploy to sell more Guinness, the book was the UK's best-seller by Christmas 1955 and is now the top-selling copyrighted series of all time.

LUTHER KING HAS A DREAM

It's inspiring to think of the difference a single day can sometimes make, and Dr Martin Luther King did nothing less than change the world on this day in 1963 when he delivered his 'I have a dream' speech.

A quarter of a million civil rights protesters gathered at the Lincoln Memorial in Washington, DC, and King didn't disappoint them. He belted out the single most famous speech in history. A technical masterclass in rhetoric, it gave the civil rights movement an unstoppable momentum and made King a human rights icon. It put pressure on the Kennedy administration to push ahead with reform, and the next year King became the youngest person to receive the Nobel Peace Prize.

WORLD BOG SNORKELLING CHAMPIONSHIP

Sometimes when life deals people lemons, they make lemonade. So when life deals people a peat bog, its obvious that what's needed is a bog snorkelling championship.

Llanwrtyd Wells is a tiny Welsh town, remarkable only for the boggyness of the nearby Waen Ryhdd swamp. Undeterred by these murky surroundings, a local mentalist today in 1985 decided to dig a sixty-yard ditch in the marsh and hold a snorkel race. Now the World Bog Snorkelling Championship is the most popular event on the bizarre sports calendar. Competitors come from around the world *even* if they have perfectly good bogs in their own gardens.

AIR GUITAR WORLD CHAMPIONSHIP

Thanks to the Air Guitar World Championship, which was first held today in 1996, there is a place where your talents of being able to do nothing are taken seriously.

What started as a few drunken jokers leaping on stage to make fools of themselves at the Oulu Music

Video Festival in Finland has now become a major international competition. Competitors are judged on three aspects of their playing: technical merit – how close they are to an actual performance of the piece; stage presence – how much rock star charisma they have; and finally, *airness* – a special something that's impossible to put your finger on. Just like an air guitar itself.

LA TOMATINA

Today the mother of all food fights occurs when the entire populace of the Spanish town of Buñol dedicate the day to throwing tomatoes at one another.

'La Tomatina' started in 1945, when disgruntled locals lobbed over-ripe fruit at politicians. This was such a laugh that they did the same thing again the next year and a tradition was born. Now up to 50,000 tourists come every year to cause chaos, swelling the tiny town to bursting point.

Shopkeepers pin up plastic to protect their storefronts, combatants strip to their swimwear and don goggles. When the battle is finished, more than 100 tons of fruit will have splattered in the streets. That's a lot of mess, but also a lot of smiling faces.

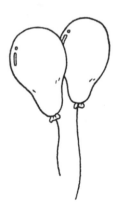

SEPTEMBER

LEGALISED GAMBLING? YOU BET!

Nowadays, bookies will happily give you odds on anything – from Elvis being alive (1,000-1) to Paris Hilton being elected President (also 1,000-1). But before the first-ever legal betting shop opened today in 1960, you couldn't even bet on a comparative dead cert like aliens existing (100-1).

The daftest-ever bet was that the world would end at 12.50p.m. on 11 August 1999, at 1,000,000-1. Even if the punter won, how did he think he was going to pick up his money?

THE SIMPSONS

On this day in 1990, two years after our US brethren, UK fans of comedy got something new to laugh at and fans of traditional family values got something new to moan about – *The Simpsons* first aired on TV.

While most of us were happy to laugh at this most dysfunctional of families, to some moral guardians, the show was a disgrace. Former First Lady Barbara Bush famously called *The Simpsons* 'the dumbest thing she had ever seen'.

Ironic, really, when you look at her family.

REDHEAD DAY

Redheads rejoice! If you're tired of being treated as a lower-class citizen, then today is your chance to revel in your russet splendour.

Just pop over to Breda, in the Netherlands, where the annual Redhead Day is now underway. There you will find yourself the centre of celebrations of all that's positive about having two recessive genes on chromosome sixteen. You can watch redheaded models showing off titian-tastic tailoring, tuck into a redhead-themed dinner and party your freckles off at an auburns-only nightclub.

Just don't forget the factor fifty in case you go down to the beach to celebrate.

NO MORE CONVICTS!

Today, in 1884, the UK ended its policy of shipping convicts to New South Wales – no more would the prisoners of one society be unfairly set loose in a land of virgin paradise.

If people in Britain had only wised up to the fact that Australia wasn't the prison-like nightmare it had been made out to be – *in fact it was the exact opposite* – the transportation of deadly prisoners wouldn't have appeared so ridiculous 200 years later. If anything, most of us would have gone freely . . .

SEALAND DECLARED LEGAL

Being king of your own country is something most men can only dream of. So let's celebrate Roy Bates today, who made that dream reality.

Roy decreed the new state of Sealand on this day in 1978. This 'nation' is actually an abandoned World War II fort six miles off the coast of Suffolk consisting of two vast tubular legs with a platform on top. Bates simply occupied it and declared himself 'Prince' Roy and his wife 'Princess' Joan.

However, after the initial fun of conquest wore off, the Bates royal family retired to Essex. Being a king is one thing, living on a concrete stump in the middle of the howling North Sea is quite another.

PIGGLY WIGGLY

Shoplifters of the world are united in their appreciation of Piggly Wiggly, the first true self-service grocery store opened in Memphis today in 1916.

Before this store opened, shopkeepers everywhere retrieved and packed each item for customers prior to their arriving. But Piggly Wiggly's *modus operandi* was to open shelves and checkout stands and put the selection of items in the hands of its customers. A revolutionary concept for its time, it was soon copied in every shop the world over.

It was also the first shop to price each item, handy for working out the worth of what you'd managed to pinch, but which also saved the poor shopkeeper from having to repeat the same bit of information 200 times a day.

LET'S ZEP

Today, in 1968, was the birth of hard rock: Messrs Plant, Page, Jones and Bonham first played together in front of a live audience and achieved something every teenage child in the world wanted – rock 'n' roll fame and glory.

There have been plenty of hard-rocking bands, but Led Zeppelin were the first to have it all. They were immensely talented musicians and had a hell of an appetite for chaos.

Stadium adulation, flared jumpsuits, motorcycles in hotels, groupies, marathon booze sessions, and their own private jet to get them to the next party – no one lived quite such a cheerful existence as these four 'golden gods'.

TO BOLDLY GO

From its boldly split infinitive in the opening credits to its disposable crewmembers and rubber-suited monsters, the original *Star Trek* TV series changed the lives of millions of geeks today in 1966, when its first episode was shown in the US.

The show also went boldly into a multi-cultural space that no show had ever gone before: the Enterprise had a black female communications officer, a Japanese helmsman, a Russian navigator and a Vulcan-Earthling first officer. And when Captain Kirk and Lieutenant Uhura locked lips it was the first interracial kiss ever shown on American TV. To boldly go, indeed . . .

COLONEL SANDERS HATCHES A PLAN

There are times when Kentucky Fried Chicken will put a mighty big smile on your face. And back on this day in 1890, the future fried-food king who started it all, Colonel Sanders, was born.

The Colonel's image is now ubiquitous, but he had to have been one of the slowest businessmen in history. He didn't get around to franchising Kentucky Fried Chicken restaurants until he was sixty five, using $105 from his first OAP payment as seed capital.

But thankfully he did. He helped revolutionise the fast-food industry by being the first to strip down his menu to just a few items.

LARGE HADRON COLLIDER

Today in 2008, science boffins fired up the most insanely-powerful particle accelerator ever. This mega-collider, a 27km ring in Switzerland, smashes proton beams (no, I don't know what they are) together in a quest to answer some of the most fundamental questions of the universe and, hopefully, discover the 'God particle' – The Higgs Boson. Finding it will prove something that is Incredibly Important, but a little tricky to explain here.

MANHATTAN DISCOVERED

Given that 11 September is now one of the world's most infamous dates, you might think there's not much to smile about today. But thanks to one of those curious quirks of history, we can fittingly celebrate the fact that today is also the day explorer Henry Hudson first came across Manhattan Island itself.

People often laugh at the fact that the local Lenape people sold what would become the world's most valuable slice of real estate to the Dutch in 1626 for goods worth sixty guilders (about $1,000 today). But, at that time, Manhattan was a rocky wilderness with a few deer wandering about. It was a pretty good deal, really.

MOST EXCITING ASHES

Today in 2005 was the final climactic day of a summer series that had even non-cricket fans on the edge of their seats. It was a glorious reminder that sport can be about more than winning and losing – occasionally it can produce a contest almost transcendentally thrilling.

The Australians had ruled the Ashes for years, and beforehand many of them had talked up the possibility of another 5–0 whitewash. But the games turned out to be some of the closest and most exciting sporting contests ever. One match was decided by just two runs. Even today, the very last day of the nine-week series, either team could have won. Finally, England did, triggering a party that was nearly as legendary.

NEXT TIME YOU HAVE A HEADACHE, SPARE A THOUGHT ...

 Today in 1848, Phineas Gage was working on a railroad in Vermont. He was compacting a charge of blasting powder using an iron rod that was 1¼in in diameter and 3ft 7in long when the powder exploded, blasting the bar into the side of his face, behind his left eye, through his brain and clean out the top of his head, to land 80ft away.

Incredibly, despite this violent intrusion to his noggin, Gage was still conscious and talking when the doctor arrived. He was pretty poorly for a few months but he recovered and went on to live for another twelve years and his case contributed immensely to the development of modern neurology.

So next time you're grumpy and have a headache, remember Mr Gage ...

LISDOONVARNA MATCHMAKING FESTIVAL

Lisdoonvarna, Ireland, is Europe's largest and oldest (150 years!) matchmaking festival, and the normally tiny town swells with 40,000 romantic hopefuls this day each year, with lots of single men and women. Organising this orgy of ogling is The Matchmaker – traditionally the person who knew all the farmers with eligible sons and daughters. He would invite them to Lisdoonvarna to meet, cashing in on the generous dowries when he successfully paired a couple off.

The festival is held in September because that was customarily when all the crops were gathered in. With the hay in the barn, lovers finally had something they could roll around in.

VIVA LA BIBA!

Biba was the store that was responsible for putting the mini-skirt on the high street. It was also the first shop to put super-hip clothes within reach of ordinary girls – what they saw on telly on a Friday night, they could buy on Saturday morning and then go out in that night. Its innovative décor, store layouts and trendy staff made clothes shopping a fashionable activity in itself, starting retail trends that are now commonplace. Not great news for shopping-phobic men, but at least they got to enjoy the mini-skirts.

TAKE-YOUR-DOG-TO-WORK-DAY

Animal charity The Blue Cross have encouraged thousands of company owners to let dogs tag along with workers today since 1996 and it's an idea that seems to work. Surveys have actually proved that staff feel more cheerful. Which makes joining in with Take-Your-Dog-To-Work Day good for your business, too – unless, of course, you own a sausage factory.

OKTOBERFEST STARTS

Munich's Oktoberfest is the world's biggest booze-up, and is renowned globally as *the* party event of the year.

The first Oktoberfest in 1810 might have been held in honour of a royal wedding, but no one can remember for certain. Now six million beer fans come every year to sink 400,000 litres of beer *a day* – the equivalent of an Olympic swimming pool full of booze.

Which probably means that 18 September is Hangover Day, but hey, who cares?

LIGHTS, BLACKPOOL...ACTION!

A spectacular light show is a great way to brighten up your day, and the most brilliant display of them all first set the skies ablaze above the north's capital city of fun today in 1879.

The first Blackpool Illuminations were just a dozen arc lamps on the Promenade, but they were still amazing – this was a full year before Thomas Edison patented the electric light bulb. Today they stretch for six miles along the seafront and use more than a million bulbs.

The other good thing about the lights is that should you have a little too much fun, they're great for finding your way back to your hotel in the middle of the night.

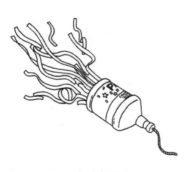

INTERNATIONAL TALK-LIKE-A-PIRATE DAY

Today's celebration of high-seas hilarity was created in 1996 by a pair of scurvy old dogs by the names of Ol' Chumbucket and Cap'n Slappy. This is not a joke.

After a British radio DJ mentioned ITLAPD on his show the day became an international phenomenon and millions of people each year celebrate the day by talking like complete buccaneers.

So when you step out of bed this morning and stub your toe, don't screech 'Ow!'; yell 'Aaaarrrr!!' When meeting your friends, forget 'hello', and bellow 'Ahoy, me hearty!' instead. You'll feel better. Oi promise ye.

BATTLE OF THE SEXES

When male ex-tennis champion Bobby Riggs challenged the 1973 Ladies Champion to a match, it was about more than tennis: 'I want Billie Jean King,' he proclaimed, 'I want the women's liberation leader!'

It was a time of sexual revolution and Riggs set himself up as the ultimate chauvinist. He wore a T-shirt that said 'Men's Liberation' and proclaimed he would demolish King simply because he was a man. An unprecedented 30,000 spectators packed the stadium in Houston and more than fifty million people were glued to their sets, ready for this ultimate battle of the sexes. Riggs egged on the crowd by entering the stadium in a carriage pulled by women.

Billie Jean King nailed him in straight sets, 6-4, 6-3, 6-3.

INTERNATIONAL DAY OF PEACE

The International Day of Peace is globally recognised today. It gives all of us a chance to demonstrate our dedication to peace. Hell, even just the absence of war would be nice.

Coincidentally, today is also International Day of Peas. This in itself should be enough to cheer you up. Peas Day is an annual celebration of legumes and greenness and is promoted by farmers, supermarkets and vegetable interest groups around the world to promote vegetable-awareness. The day is especially hilarious because it gives all of us a chance to say the line . . . 'give peas a chance'.

HOBBIT DAY

Today is the birthday of Bilbo and Frodo Baggins, the hobbit stars of J. R. R. Tolkien's books *The Hobbit* and *The Lord of the Rings* trilogy. This is particularly important to Tolkiendils (fans) because the epic action in *The Lord of the Rings* kicks off with Bilbo's 'eleventy-first' birthday party. Gandalf sees that Bilbo is being affected by the One Ring and realises it must be destroyed, marking the start of Frodo's quest. All over the world people gather to celebrate today in a hobbitty way: by hosting parties, sharing feasts and readings from the book.

BISEXUALITY DAY

If you were allowed to choose your sexual orientation, many people would happily plump for bisexual. It doubles your chances of finding a partner, doesn't it?

Actually, it was exactly that sort of attitude as to why today was established back in 1999. Bisexuals were tired of being stigmatised as indecisive, so they set up a day of information and celebration to finally set the sexual record straight.

FEAST OF THE INGATHERING

As long as man has been harvesting the bounty of nature he has also been marking the time around the autumn equinox with much celebration. In many English counties, this merriment was increased by the harvesters electing a 'Lord' from among themselves. During the harvest, the Lord was to be obeyed at all times, on pain of a fine – usually an alcoholic drink. At the end of the day's harvesting, a drinking horn had to pass in a strict order, from the Harvest Lord to his men.

Add a few more rules and some strong continental lager and you have the basis of many drinking games still popular to this day. Ducky Fuzz, anyone?

FERRARA BALLOON FESTIVAL

The Ferrara Balloon Festival is the biggest and most fun ballooning event in the world. Gaze in wonder at the crazy balloons in all sorts of odd shapes and sizes, from a leaping cow to Darth Vader's helmet, a bottle of champagne or even an enormous bumblebee. Enjoy balloon races, kite displays, concerts, or take off on a flight of your own over the stunningly beautiful Italian city. It happens this day every year so there's no excuse not to go is there?

FISH HAVE FINGERS?

Fishfingers are one of life's greatest comfort foods. And they only came about by accident. Britain's herring producers in 1955 were looking for a new way of boosting sales, so they created a battered and crumbed herring finger called 'herring savouries' first sold today. To make these even more appealing to shoppers they introduced a bland control product made from cod. Unfortunately for them, fish-fans flipped for the cod version instead of the herring, and their trade took even more of a battering – by 1965, cod fishfingers made up ten per cent of Britain's entire fish consumption.

CONVENIENCE TO A T

Car No. 0001 of the historic line of Model T automobiles rolled out of Ford's Piquette Plant in Detroit today in 1908.

The car didn't just bring wide-open spaces within the reach of millions of modernising families, it helped Henry Ford perfect his revolutionary 'production line' method of manufacture. Ford eventually made production so efficient that it took just ninety three minutes to assemble a Model T. Its simplicity and affordable price made it an incredible success – by 1918, Model Ts accounted for half of all cars in America.

FLEMINICILLIN

'When I woke up just after dawn on September 28, 1928, I certainly didn't plan to revolutionise all medicine by discovering the world's first antibiotic, or bacteria killer. But I guess that was exactly what I did'.

These were the precise words of Alexander Fleming. Fleming was just back from a month's holiday. He'd been studying bacteria and hadn't tidied up before he left. He turned to a stack of sample dishes in a corner and noticed that one culture was contaminated with a fungus. The colonies of bacteria around it were dead. That mould turned out to be penicillin, the most efficacious life-saving drug ever known.

Proof that being a bit of a slob can pay off.

BRITAIN'S FIRST CURRY HOUSE

If you're a fan of a nice 'n' spicy curry, today you should raise a cold glass of Kingfisher to Dean Mahomet, the man who brought the biryani to Britain.

He opened the UK's first Indian restaurant, the Hindoostanee Coffee House, on this day in 1809. It was aimed at the aristocracy, promising a place to 'enjoy the Hookha with real Chilm tobacco and Indian dishes of the highest perfection'. Unfortunately, London's toffs weren't ready for rogan josh, and the venture soon closed.

But Mahomet had planted a (cumin) seed in the public's bellies and in the years to come, many more Indian eateries opened. Today there are more than 9,000 curry houses in the UK – yum!

'TENNIS GIRL' POSTER

For men of a certain vintage this was *the* poster of their youth – a young woman stand at a tennis net in the hazy summer sunshine completely commando.

Well, this iconic image was captured today in 1976 at the University of Birmingham. The eighteen-year-old model was the photographer's then-girlfriend. You could say that the poster's popularity was due to what it symbolised: a fleeting moment of youthful beauty; the sunshine and sex of the 1970s; a post-modern reaction to feminism.

But at the end of the day, you can't get away from the fact that she simply had a very fine bottom.

OCTOBER

DISNEY WORLD

If a theme park twice the size of Manhattan sounds like lots of fun, then Walt Disney World in Florida – which opened its doors today in 1971 – is the place for you.

It's the biggest and most popular resort on the planet, a massive paradise for the young and young at heart. Happy kids of all ages chomp their way through nearly 2 miles of hot dogs here every single day. It has four theme parks, two water parks, and so many hotel rooms it would take you 68 years to sleep in them all.

But by far the most glorious thing about Disney World is that in 2009 it was twinned with ... wait for it ... Swindon.

FIRST TELEVISION TRANSMISSION

Television brings a non-stop carousel of drama, news and celebrity 'entertainment' into our homes. And it's all thanks to John Logie Baird who successfully sent the first television picture on this day in 1925.

Not everyone in the world was wowed at the potential for visual wonderment that this invention presented. When Baird visited the *Daily Express* to rustle up some PR, the editor was petrified. He yelped at a colleague: 'For God's sake, go down to reception and get rid of a lunatic who's down there. He says he's got a machine for seeing by wireless! Watch him – he may have a razor on him'.

TEA RATIONING ENDS

How would you feel if every tea bag had to last for five cups? Not so happy, I'll bet. So you can understand how cheerful everyone in Britain must have been today in 1952 when the government finally announced the end of tea rationing.

It had been twelve years since any British person had been allowed to pop as many bags in the pot as they pleased. They must have been gasping. The only grey cloud on the horizon was that it would be another full year until biscuits were off the ration books as well.

REMOTE LEARNING ... BY DONKEY

On his deathbed, St Francis of Assisi thanked his donkey for a life of help, and his donkey apparently wept. But since donkeys are never usually celebrated, we've chosen St Francis' Feast Day to do so, and to tell the touching tale of the *biblioburro*.

This remarkable mobile library brings books to an impoverished community on the backs of two donkeys. Colombian teacher Luis Soriano loads books into panniers on the backs of his *burros*, Alfa and Beto. He started in the late 1990s with seventy books but now, thanks to donations, has more than 4,800.

And, of course, all late fines are payable in carrots.

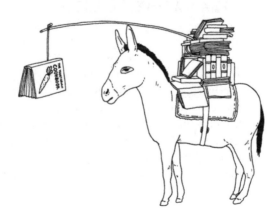

MONTY PYTHON

Life changed for the sillier today in 1969 when Monty Python's first TV show *And Now For Something Completely Different* first aired and blew traditional comedy out of the water.

Today's first episode included 'The Funniest Joke in the World', a classic sketch about a joke so amusing that anyone who hears it will die laughing. In a fittingly surreal way, the Pythons were so funny they actually managed this feat. In 1989, a Danish audiologist, Ole Bentzen, died laughing while watching *A Fish Called Wanda*, the film by Pythons John Cleese and Michael Palin.

Which is sad, but at least his last moments were cheerful.

FIRST PLANET OUTSIDE OUR SOLAR SYSTEM

Today in 1995 was a great day for extraterrestrial spotters. With more than 100 billion stars, our galaxy is a cosmic haystack, but astronomers finally found the first planet orbiting a star other than our own sun.

The good news is that Bellerophon, as this new planet is called, is 'only' fifty light years from Earth. So if there are any aliens living there, they don't have far to come to visit us.

The bad news is that the planet is extremely close to its sun, has a surface temperature of 1,000°C and three times the gravity of Earth. So our nearest neighbours are likely to be giant radioactive slugs.

SWEDISH TWINS INVADE ENGLAND

So, you've popped into town to pick up some sausages on a wet October Friday in 1997, when all of a sudden ninety sets of Swedish identical twins giggle past. Nice.

The twins, it turns out, were taking part in a 'science experiment' in Stockholm, when the scientists decided they needed a break. So they were all packed off on a chartered ferry for a 'day of fun' in Felixstowe. Mischievously, no one told the locals.

It makes me smile to imagine the looks on shoppers' faces as pair after pair of striking Scandinavian siblings dressed in identical outfits walked by. They must have thought they were being invaded by a weird clone army of some sort.

THE MICROWAVE

Nuking your dinner might not be that healthy, but it's damn handy (especially if you're drunk). And so today we thank radar researcher Dr Percy Spencer for some instant gratification.

Percy was mucking about with a magnetron when he noticed that the bar of chocolate in his pocket had melted. Rather than turning the machine off and leaving the room immediately, as any sensible person would have done, Percy got hold of some popcorn and fired the thing up again. When the kernels popped, he realised he may have just invented something revolutionary – at least in the meals-for-one market. And on this day in 1945 he filed the patent for the first-ever microwave oven.

WORLD CONKER CHAMPIONSHIPS

In an age when more and more fun traditions are being outlawed for health and safety reasons, it's good to see that some people are still taking their fun seriously.

The people of Ashton, Northamptonshire don't care what the grumps say – today they'll be hosting the World Conker Championships on their village green.

If you fancy your chances this year, head down to Ashton and lace up. Here's a tip: a dense conker is a good conker. You can test this by dropping your chestnut into water. If it floats, toss it. If it sinks, it's a beaut.

WOODMAS

Ed Wood Jr is regarded as a dreadful film director. But his films are *so* bad he inspired his own religion, the Church of Ed Wood. It has over 3,500 baptised followers and today you can join them on their greatest festivity, Woodmas, held to celebrate Ed's birthday.

In real life Ed was a transvestite with an angora sweater fetish. He served in the marines during World War II, and fought in the Battle of Guadalcanal wearing a bra and panties under his uniform.

MARY ROSE

The Mary Rose was a large ship commissioned by Henry VIII to establish a new era for the Royal Navy. It was sunk by a freak wind while turning in the Solent. It then lay at the bottom of the sea until today's rescue mission in 1982. This hugely complex operation lifted the wreck in a massive steel structure, which cradled the ship as its jagged timbers were inched above the surface for the first time in over 400 years.

Pretty boring to watch, yes, but there was one great bit where the frame broke and totally crunched into the ship.

WINSTON CHURCHILL'S SPECIAL BREW

Today in 1950, Churchill had just completed a three-day trip to Denmark. To commemorate the visit of the famously strong leader, Carlsberg brewed an equally formidable beer – Special Brew. At 9% ABV, it was one of the most potent beers around, but Churchill enjoyed it so much he later sent a thank you letter and had two crates of it delivered to his London home.

Indeed, Churchill was famous for enjoying a brew or two. When told off by a lady for being tipsy, he famously replied: 'I may be drunk, Miss, but in the morning I will be sober and you will still be ugly'.

WHERE ON EARTH?

Telling someone how to get from A to B is pretty hard if you don't agree on where A is. Obvious, but this was a big problem before this day in 1884.

The trouble was the prime meridian – an imaginary line around the Earth that's essential to navigation. French and English maps used different meridians. And so did twenty other countries. So a conference was held to finally decide on a universal meridian. Greenwich got the vote because most maps already used it.

This was great for getting ships to where they should be, but best of all it annoyed the French intensely. They went into a huff and continued to use the Paris Meridian until 1911 for timekeeping and until 1914 for navigation.

WINNIE-THE-POOH

Published today in 1926, the adventures of Pooh has cheered up millions of children for generations. And even more wonderfully, it's a story that is completely and utterly true. And I can prove it.

The Hundred Acre Wood is based on Ashdown Forest in Sussex – you can even identify real forest views from the illustrations. The boy in the story is based on the author's own son, Christopher Robin Milne, and the animals on his stuffed toys. Christopher's bear was named after Winnie, a black bear he used to visit at London Zoo. The 'Pooh' bit comes from a swan that went by that name.

The stuffed animal toys currently reside in the former New York Public Library Main Branch in New York. You can visit them there, if you like. Just remember to bring plenty of hunny.

STADIUM WAVES

15

Joining in a stadium wave is great fun, unless of course the person next to you has a full beer. But if you'd tried doing it before this day in 1981, everyone would have just thought you'd had a few too many yourself.

This very first wave was not invented in Mexico, but in Edmonton, Canada, and it was accidental. A cheerleader called Krazy George was trying to organise a bit of support from the crowd at an ice hockey game and one section of fans was

slow to respond to his calls. Then the next section was also delayed, and so a wave went slowly rolling around the arena out of sync. But George saw potential for a mass wave and when he was called on to lead the cheer at a major-league baseball game in Oakland, he coaxed the curious crowd into producing the first televised wave on this day in 1981.

THE FEMALE KING OF POLAND

Don't let a small thing like being the wrong gender stop you from achieving your goals. Jadwiga was crowned *King* of Poland today in 1384 and *she* was a *woman*.

The Poles were very particular in officially crowning her 'King' not 'Queen', because they wanted to ensure she was respected as a monarch in her own right and not just a royal consort. She seems to have been quite a popular king. She led two successful military expeditions and married the Grand Duke of Lithuania. (No, he didn't become a queen.)

THE LONDON BEER FLOOD

If you've ever had a drunken idea that went wrong, take heart – there's no chance it went as wrong as today's event in 1814 at the Meux's Horse Shoe Brewery in London's West End.

The brewery was so proud of its vast new brewing vat (twenty two feet tall and sixty feet in diameter) that it held an inauguration dinner inside it for 200 people. They then filled the vat but, alas, it ruptured. Several other vats exploded, the building caved in and a 'brew-nami' of 1.3 million gallons of beer flooded down Tottenham Court Road. Nine people perished by 'drowning, injury, poisoning by the porter fumes, or drunkenness'.

This might seem a little sad, but we've all got to go sometime, and there are worse ways that under a wave of beer.

CHRISTMAS CRACKERED

For over 160 years the Cracker has been one of our most popular Christmas traditions.

Today in 1847, entrepreneur Tom Smith took the idea of the French *bon bon*, a sugared almond wrapped in a twist of tissue paper, up-sized it and added a 'banging' bit of paper for good measure. He made a fortune and his name still appears on the most famous brand of crackers today.

THE FIRST DISCOTHÈQUE AND DJ

None of the wonders of the modern disco would exist today if it weren't for what German journalist Klaus Quirini did on this particular day in 1959.

Decades ago, dancehalls always used a live band to fill their floors. Anything else simply hadn't been done. When, one night, the booked band didn't show up at the Scotch Club in Aachen, Germany, Klaus took it upon himself to stick a simple LP player in the corner of the room and start entertaining the crowd with songs, announcements and audience-participation games. This was a revolutionary idea and Klaus' style became popular. The discothèque, and the modern DJ, were born.

LIGHTS! CAMERA! BIGFOOT!

Truth is a wonderful thing, but mystery is where real fun lies. Roger Patterson was out in the north Californian woods on this unspectacular day in 1967 when something seemingly spectacular happened. He filmed on tape an unidentifiable species of giant ape, seven-and-a-half-feet tall, with short black hair over its body and large breasts. You've seen it.

He claimed it was genuine 'Bigfoot' footage, but many experts have cited much proof of its fakery, namely:

1) A large species of ape could not live unobserved for so long

in one of the most populated states in America.

2) Roger Patterson was a well known Bigfoot fanatic.

3) It looks like a guy in a monkey suit.

BATTLE OF TRAFALGAR

It was the famous naval victory today in 1805 that saw off the rascally French and Spanish fleets from our shores. It also established Trafalgar Day, still a big celebration in many Commonwealth navies. And it saw the creation of what has to be history's ickiest cocktail . . .

Britain's hero Nelson was killed during the battle. To preserve his body for burial back in England, Nelson's second-in-command popped the dead body into the ship's rum supply and banned all liquor rations to the crew. When the ship reached port, however, the vat was dry . . . the thirsty seamen had been secretly drinking from it. Naval rum was henceforth known as Nelson's Blood.

Talk about getting pickled . . .

FIRST PARACHUTE JUMP

You have to admire the nutters of this world.

Take André-Jacques Garnerin, an adrenaline junkie of the eighteenth century. It had only been a few years since the first successful balloon flight when, on this day in 1797, he decided to quite simply jump out of one and entrust his life to a *never-used-before* piece of silk as a parachute.

Landing successfully to great adulation (this entry wouldn't be very cheerful if he hadn't), he made the name of Garnerin even more famous by encouraging his wife to become the first ever female parachutist.

THE BIRTH OF ALL CREATION...APPARENTLY

As celebrations go, today ought to be a biggy – the entire universe, it seems, was created today in 4004 BC.

At least it was according to the seventeenth century divine James Ussher. After a thorough study of the Bible and other ancient texts, he calculated that the first day in all history was 23 October 4004 BC.

The idea for his calculation was sound, given that the Bible was read as gospel. Working backwards from Adam to Solomon (and with a bit of cross-referencing for later gaps) he was able to work out the precise moment when all life supposedly came into being. Conveniently, this was a Sunday.

NIAGARA IN A BARREL

Next time you're a bit upset, cheer up – you'll probably never have to go to the lengths Annie Taylor did on this day in 1901.

Annie's husband and only child had died. She hadn't had a job in years. How was she going to get the money she needed to fund her dotage? Simple. She'd become the first person to go over Niagara Falls in a barrel.

Annie was set adrift on the day of her sixty third birthday, with only a small mattress and her lucky pillow for company.

Swept over the Horseshoe Falls she plummeted 173 feet into the maelstrom below. Twenty minutes later, the aged adventuress was found a little dazed but alive. Fifteen people have gone over Niagara in a barrel since Annie. Five died.

MONSTER PUNCH

A big bowl of heftily-spiked punch will lift the spirits of any party, but the punch prepared on this day in 1694 must have sent guests practically into orbit.

It was prepared by Admiral Edward Russell, commander of Britain's Mediterranean fleet, at Alicante. Rather than use a bowl for his punch, Russell employed a huge marble fountain. Into this went 200 gallons of brandy, 100 gallons of Malaga wine, 20 gallons of lime juice, 2,500 lemons, half a ton of sugar, 5lbs of grated nutmegs, 300 toasted biscuits, and 400 gallons of water. A boy in a rowing boat floated around in it filling the guests' cups.

The party continued until the vast fountain had been drunk dry – seven days later.

MRS BEETON

When her *Book of Household Management* was published on this day in 1861, Mrs Isabella Beeton started a revolution . . . and set *the* template for the modern cookbook. For the first time ever, recipes included ingredients at the start and were illustrated with coloured engravings. As well as recipes, the book also covered household topics like dealing with servants' pay – this might not be much use to you and me, but is probably quite handy for today's super-rich celebrity chefs.

AMSTERDAM FOUND

It's the city that brings cheer in so many ways: architecture, museums, canals, flower markets, cosmopolitan locals. Oh, and cannabis cafés and legalised prostitution. The only city on Earth that does, lest we forget.

The city's more than *laissez faire* approach to life has always been part of daily routine in Amsterdam. The city's name first appeared on a certificate dated this day in 1275 – which exempted the locals from paying a fee to cross the Amstel River. This was the making of the city – it boosted trade and helped grow the young settlement into the trading and cultural metropolis it is today.

SNOW GLOBE

Snow globes were first sold at the Paris World's Fair on this day in 1878. Not overly exciting, you may think, but this exhibition was designed to celebrate the recovery of France after the brutal 1870 Franco-Prussian War. It was a time of hope, brotherhood, renewed prosperity – bizarrely symbolised by a transparent glass bubble filled with water, a twee landscape and bits of floaty white stuff.

SCOTCH EGG

If it weren't for Fortnum & Mason, which opened its doors today in 1707, we wouldn't have that staple of the motorway service station, the Scotch egg – the delicacy was invented there.

Indeed, the Piccadilly-based super-pantry has a history populated with eccentrics and rogues. It was founded by a royal footman who used it as an outlet to sell candles that he stole from Buckingham Palace and was the first shop in Britain to stock Heinz baked beans – an expensive imported delicacy in the 1930s.

MISCHIEF NIGHT

Mischief Night, or Devil's Night, dates back to 1790 and its eerie origins lay in the legend of Guy Fawkes and Halloween. Today though it is an extremely popular day in the calendars of British and American youngsters who use it to prank upstanding members of the community – toilet-papering their houses, throwing eggs, stealing street signs and acting basically like ASBO hooligans ... but with an excuse.

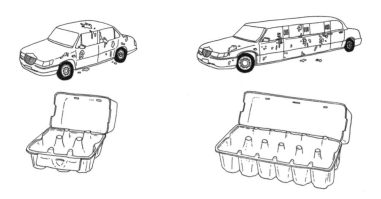

SAMHAIN

Modern Halloween's traditional rituals actually date back to the ancient Celtic festival of Samhain. Marking the start of the darker half of the year, Samhain was a time when cattle were slaughtered to set aside a store of meat for the winter. (The word 'bonfire' comes from 'bone-fire' – what happens to the remnants of the unlucky beasts.) It was also a night when the border between our world and the netherworld became thin and spirits could float between the two worlds more freely. So to keep the evil spirits at bay, young men would don costumes and masks to scare off any supernatural terrors with bad intentions. Nowadays, kids just vandalise your car if you don't give them sweets.

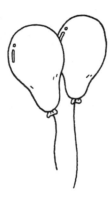

NOVEMBER

DAY OF THE DEAD

Death can be a bit of a downer, but not today in Mexico. This annual 'Day of the Dead' festival is over 3,000 years old, and although the Spanish Conquistadors tried to stamp it out, the indigenous people stood their ground. The day is all about celebrating and re-telling anecdotes about the faithfully departed making it a triumphantly cheerful festival of all that's great about being alive.

THE FIRST CHEERLEADER

When University of Minnesota football fan Johnny Campbell stood up today in 1898 and shouted 'Rah, Rah, Rah! Sku-u-mar, Hoo-Rah! Hoo-Rah! Varsity! Varsity! Varsity, Minn-e-So-Tah!' most people in the crowd probably though he was a drunk moron. Those who didn't copied his cheerful chant and Campbell has since gone down in history as the very first cheerleader.

BIRTH OF THE (EARL OF) SANDWICH

It's not like you wouldn't have anything for lunch today if it weren't for the Fourth Earl of Sandwich (born today in 1718); someone else would surely have had the idea of putting a piece of meat in between two slices of bread. But your meal would most certainly be called something else.

And it's a good job the Earl's favourite snack was named after his title, rather than his surname, or you would be having a cheese and ham Montagu for lunch.

O-BA-MA!

Hundreds of thousands of people in America hit the streets to celebrate a new chapter in history as Barack Obama became President today in 2008.

After 43 white guys in a row, Obama was the first person of colour to be elected to America's highest office and was a man who genuinely looked like he could offer a radical change.

Not many people know it, but Obama once went on a stag night in Wokingham when his half-sister married an Englishman. He left before the stripper took to the stage, but still, what a legend.

GUY FAWKES NIGHT

Officially, tonight's bonfires and fireworks celebrate the foiling of the Gunpowder Plot of 1605 in which Catholic conspirators, including Guy Fawkes, attempted to blow up the Houses of Parliament. They wanted to shatter Protestant rule by detonating the Houses of Parliament whilst King James I and the entire aristocracy were inside. These nobles were saved at the eleventh hour when Fawkes was caught in the cellars with 1,800 pounds of gunpowder and the seventeenth century equivalent of a Zippo lighter.

SAX AND THE SOUSA

The invention of a new instrument opens up a whole world of musical possibilities. And today we cheer not one, but two new musical inventors – for, coincidentally, both Antoine-Joseph Sax and John Philip Sousa blew their first breaths on this day in 1814.

The saxophone has become instrumental in creating the definitive jazz sound, as well as early rock 'n' roll, big band music and ska. The sousaphone is a type of tuba that fits around the body, and is very popular in marching bands. However, Mr Sousa also composed 'The Liberty Bell' – the iconic, cheering theme that plays during the credits of *Monty Python's Flying Circus*.

JESUS SAVES

They say God moves in mysterious ways, and that was certainly true today in 1907 when a man named Jesús saved the town of Nacozari de Garcia, Mexico, from a burning train full of dynamite.

Okay, so it was Jesús García a railroad engineer – not Christ the Messiah – but what he did was still pretty brilliant. Jesús noticed a fire on a train hauling dynamite heading towards the town. Quickly, he took control of the train, at full-steam, and steered it away from danger. He ordered the fireman to jump – and just in time too. The train exploded.

Jesús had saved Nacozari de Garcia from devestating catastrophe – alas, he perished in his heroic action. But presumably he was back behind the tender three days later.

X-RAY!

Willhelm Rontgen's discovery of the X-ray today in 1895 changed the world and earnt him the Nobel Prize in 1901. With hundreds of medical applications, from finding bone breaks to diagnosing lung problems, the number of people his discovery has helped treat and cure must run into the billions.

THE FALL OF THE WALL

The TV images were incredible – a guy with a sledgehammer was knocking lumps out of the Berlin Wall as mass crowds cheered. This hated symbol of repression tumbled today in 1989 and the world was suddenly filled with hope and optimism.

The fall of the wall led to some wonderful celebrations, including David Hasselhoff's performance of his song 'Looking for Freedom' while actually standing on the wall. At that precise moment, communism in Germany well and truly became history.

STANLEY FINDS LIVINGSTONE

Today in 1871, after eight months of hacking his way through 700 miles of Tanzanian jungle, Henry Stanley eventually found Dr David Livingstone – the famous missionary who had been lost in the depths of Africa for six years. Upon finding his man, he doffed his hat, extended his hand and uttered the line, 'Dr Livingstone, I presume?'

It wasn't a particularly great day for Livingstone, of course, whose lifestyle had made it abundantly clear that he didn't actually want to be found.

FLAT HAT CLUB

Established at the College of William and Mary in Virginia, on this day in 1750, the Flat Hat Club was the first frat house – the subject of many beloved film comedies like *Animal House* and *Old School*.

Of course, it was all a bit more high-brow in those days. The society was called the 'Flat Hat Club' after the mortarboard caps then worn by all students. The toga parties, beer chugging and hazing initiations came in during the 1970s.

WORLD WIDE WEB

The Internet is all very well (see 1 January), but it's made much better with the World Wide Web – created today in 1990.

It was the bright idea of Tim Berners-Lee who was working at CERN (also home of the Large Hadron Collider, see 10 september), where the first Web site went online in 1991. He also designed and built the first Web browser.

Happily, Berners-Lee made his ideas freely available. He didn't patent anything and has never received a royalty. Had a less altruistic person created the Web, our information technology might be very, very different.

ROBERT LOUIS STEVENSON

As well as being one of literature's most influential books, *Dr Jekyll and Mr Hyde* must go down as the most spectacular beating of writer's block in history.

Author Robert Louis Stevenson was a frail man. During one bout of illness he was prescribed a hefty dose of cocaine (then a popular remedy) and retired to bed. He had a wild dream of 'a fine bogey tale'. He then used more cocaine to fuel a marathon three-day writing session in which he wrote the entire novel. But he didn't think much of that draft, so he rewrote it entirely in the next three days.

It's amusing to think that one of Victorian literature's most revered novels, published today in 1886, was written, effectively, on a six-day cocaine bender.

BOONIE'S FIRST INNINGS

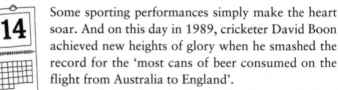

Some sporting performances simply make the heart soar. And on this day in 1989, cricketer David Boon achieved new heights of glory when he smashed the record for the 'most cans of beer consumed on the flight from Australia to England'.

Boon hadn't intended to go for the record (Rod Marsh: 46 cans not out) but when the plane left Singapore he'd already opened can number 23 (not including three at Sydney airport). By London, Boon had quaffed an astonishing 50 cans. He then had three pints at a sponsor's cocktail party and finally went to bed for 36 hours.

He made more than 500 runs that series, averaging over 70.

A DARK AND STARRY NIGHT ...

Today in 2008 saw Galloway Forest Park in Scotland recognised as one of the world's best stargazing locations. Miles from the light pollution of big cities, its acres of hills and woods boast pitch-black night skies. In a city you can only see a few hundred stars, even on the darkest of nights. But at Galloway you can see an incredible 7,000 stars.

ANGEL FALLS

It's wonderful to think that the world's highest waterfall hadn't been seen by anyone living outside a single Venezuelan jungle valley until today in 1933. That's when American pilot Jimmie Angel flew over it while looking for mineral deposits.

Although, apparently', Venezuelan explorer Ernesto Sanchez La Cruz spotted the falls in 1912, he just forget to tell anybody. How they slipped his mind is baffling: pouring off the top of an immense sandstone cliff, the stunning cascade is 3,212 feet high, 400 feet wide and the plunging water pounds itself into a spectacular mist as it crashes into the rocks below.

INTERNATIONAL STUDENTS' DAY

Today is an international observance of the positivity of student action, celebrating their major achievements over the years: the Tiananmen Square protests against Chinese state authoritarianism in 1989, the May 1968 strikes in France that rocked Charles de Gaulle's government, the Athens Polytechnic uprising against the military junta in 1973 . . . and the positioning of a traffic cone on top of Nelson's column in 1992.

AERIAL PETTING – ENDS IN WETTING

If you've ever enjoyed a bunk-up in a Boeing's bath-room, you should join today's honorary flyby for the pilot and design engineer Lawrence Sperry who founded the Mile High Club on this day in 1916.

Early high-fliers couldn't get up to any high-jinks because they had to keep their hands on the controls of the plane. Mr Sperry got around this by inventing the autopilot in 1914. And as he was demonstrating its prowess to a Mrs. Waldo Polk she apparently became so excited that the two of them enjoyed the world's first bout of aeronautical amorousness.

WORLD TOILET DAY

Whether you're in there to read the paper, take time out from your visiting mother-in-law, or even just use the facilities like a normal person, the loo is a wonderful place that deserves to be celebrated.

Today is also a charity day that aims to kick up a stink about the global sanitation crisis. A staggering 2.5 billion people don't have a proper place to go to the lavatory. This isn't just bad for hygiene, it also means they don't have anywhere to keep books like this one.

UNIVERSAL CHILDREN'S DAY

Today's celebration was first proclaimed by the United Nations General Assembly in 1954, aiming to 'encourage all countries to institute a day, firstly to promote mutual exchange and understanding among children and secondly to initiate action to benefit and promote the welfare of the world's children'.

The yo-yo was also patented on this day in 1866, which is a rather sweet coincidence, although any modern child reared on the streets of *Grand Theft Auto* is about as likely to be interested in a yo-yo as they are a bag of gravel.

WORLD HELLO DAY

Today's idea is simple: by greeting others in friendship, we send a message to world leaders that they need to use communication rather than force to settle conflicts.

Thankfully, this isn't a silly idea started by a greetings card company, but a serious attempt at improved communication. World Hello Day was started in 1973 after the Yom Kippur War and now 180 countries around the planet hold some sort of observance, so why not join in. Say 'hello' today . . .

ROBIN HOOD EXISTS

It would be nice to think that there really was a Robin Hood, robbing from the rich, giving to the poor and hiding out in Sherwood Forest – but it can't really be true, can it?

One ballad recalls how King Edward II once went to Sherwood disguised as a monk to seek the outlaw. Robin duly robbed him, but had the decency to ask him to dinner. Robin then discovered the ruse and begged his ruler's forgiveness. Edward was so charmed that he took Robin into his service.

But it seems Robin pined for his wild life and the King accepted his leave. This all sounds like fiction, except for the historical fact that in King Edward's household expenses there is an entry on this day in 1324:

To Robyn Hod, by command, owing to his being unable any longer to work, the sum of 5s.

JUKEBOX

Listening to music in a pub wouldn't be possible if it weren't for the Nickel-in-the-Slot machine that went into operation today in 1889 in the Palais Royale Saloon in San Francisco. This contraption was an Edison cylinder-style phonograph with a coin mechanism bolted on. It had no amplification and music fans had to stick their ear to a listening tube to hear their chosen tune. Despite its primitiveness, it earned over $1,000 in its first six months of operation – about £16,000 today.

THE DAN COOPER HIJACK

Holding planes to ransom is not normally a cheery thing to do and something I wouldn't usually celebrate. But today's hijack is an exception, because it's also pretty cool.

On this day in 1971, a passenger registered as Dan Cooper passed a stewardess a note claiming he had a bomb in his briefcase. A glimpse of cylinders, wires and a battery convinced her he was for real and the authorities agreed to meet his demands for $200,000. The plane landed, the cash was handed over and the hostages released. The plane took off again and during a severe storm, Cooper lowered the rear stairs, strapped on a parachute and leapt into the thunder at more than 200 miles per hour.

No one has seen him, or the money, since.

THE INVENTOR OF DYNAMITE FINDS PEACE

Alfred Nobel's invention of dynamite made him *very* rich but didn't make him cheerful.

Then in 1888 Alfred's older brother died, and a French newspaper mistakenly ran an obituary of Alfred Nobel instead, calling him, rather unsettlingly, the 'merchant of death'.

Nobel was so shocked at his public perception that he decided to set up the prizes that bear his name – in a hope to clear his reputation. It worked. The Nobel Prize – founded today – honours those who advance the fields of peace, science and literature, and the work of the many brilliant Nobel laureates over the past century has advanced mankind beyond the expectation of all.

ASTERON HOAX

One of the best media hijackings in history happened today in 1977 when an eerie voice accompanied by a deep buzzing noise completely overrode the audio of ITN's early-evening news so that ITN's Ivor Mills apparently told viewers that he was 'Asteron, an authorised representative of the Intergalactic Mission'.

Asteron then told Earth people that 'all your weapons of evil must be destroyed'. He added that we have only a short time to learn to live together in peace and that if we were unable to do so, we would have to 'leave the galaxy'.

The transmission then cut to a cartoon. Although called a hoax, no pranksters have ever been found. So what if Asteron is real . . . ?

A FACE-OFF IN FRANCE

Today in 2005, Isabelle Dinoire had her face surgically replaced by a donor from a dead person – the first face transplant ever. Her original features had tragically been ravaged by her pet dog. Before the operation she was unable to eat or speak, but after she could do both. The surgical team were pioneers in their techniques and medical history had solved another unbelievable-but-true case. Whatever next?

VOTES FOR WOMEN

New Zealand was well ahead of the game when it was the first country to give women the vote on this day in 1893 – Britain didn't follow suit for another thirty five years.

Ironically enough, the legislation for suffrage was speeded on its way by a sexist man putting his foot in it. New Zealand's Premier, Richard Seddon, disliked the idea of woman's rights, and decided to stop the bill. He ordered one of his own councillors to change his vote. However, two other councillors were so angered at Seddon manipulating matters that they promptly changed sides. The bill passed by twenty votes to eighteen and opened a new era of equal rights. The world took notice . . .

PONG

In 1972 two young computer geeks built a simple electronic tennis game called *Pong*, using an old telly, a cheap wooden cabinet and some home-soldered electronics. No big manufacturers were remotely interested so the inventors decided to put the prototype in a local bar beside the jukebox.

The bar owner called later in the week saying the game wasn't working. The problem turned out to be simple: the machine was jammed and overflowing with money.

The company run by the two friends was called Atari, and they had just created the video game industry.

SHOPS COME CLEAN

If someone sells you a toupée on the basis it is 'undetectable' it really ought to be – that's pretty fundamental to the whole idea. So it's a very good thing, particularly for bald men, that the Trade Descriptions Act came into force on this day in 1968.

Before today, traders were in the habit of exaggerating their products' powers quite a lot – the Board of Trade found washable bell-bottom trousers that were completely unwashable and a nine pence cup of tea that cost one shilling and thruppence. But thanks to this day traders could no longer promise any old tat on a sign in a window and take someone's cash without delivering the advertised goods.

DECEMBER

ROSA PARKS STAYS SEATED

Rosa Parks' bus journey home from work today in 1955 changed the world. After a long, tiring day and faced with a bus full of people Rosa decided to sit down. When the bus driver asked her to stand so that a white man could sit down (as was the law then) Rosa decided that the law was wrong and remained seated.

Unfortunately, the driver didn't agree. Rosa was arrested and fined $10. She appealed and, due to the timing and high public profile of the case, racial segregation on buses was soon outlawed by the Supreme Court. Rosa was hailed as an icon of the burgeoning civil rights movement.

THRILLER

Michael Jackson may have been madder than a bag of badgers, but he certainly knew how to entertain people. When his music video for the song 'Thriller' came out today in 1983, it changed pop music forever.

Everything about it is insanely ambitious. It's fourteen minutes long, for a start, cost more than $1 million and was directed by John Landis, the hottest movie director in the world at the time. The concept and execution of the whole thing was revolutionary and has spawned countless imitators.

FIRST HEART TRANSPLANT

Today in 1967, a team headed by Christiaan Barnard popped open the chest of fifty-three-year-old Louis Washkansky, cut his heart out and put in that of a twenty-four-year old – who had hours earlier died from a car accident. Unfortunately, Mr Washkanksy only lived for eighteen days after the operation, but since then the procedure for transplants has improved considerably. One transplant patient survived for thirty one years after his operation, while another, Kelly Perkins, went on to climb Mounts. Fuji and Kilimanjaro.

REMOTE CONTROL

Whenever you channel hop or mute an infuriating advert, say a quiet thank you to inventor Robert Adler, who perfected the wireless TV remote control today in 1956.

There had been a remote-control device before Adler's, but it had used a flash of visible light. This meant that every time you switched on a lamp, you changed the channel. Adler's remote – called the Zenith Space Command – used high-pitched sound instead. This proved much more effective, although it did tend to confuse nearby bats.

PROHIBITION REPEALED

After being unable to raise a boozy cheer for more than thirteen years, Americans could finally fill their glasses on this day in 1933 when the Twenty First Amendment repealed Prohibition.

Of course, booze had been readily available throughout this period of official abstinence. In 1925 there were as many as 100,000 'speakeasies' in New York. It turned out that banning alcohol only made people want it more, and that outlawing it only served to increase the power of those who would exploit it. Still, if you need a reason to have a drink today – this is a good one!

ROYAL OIL

6

Studies reported today in 1994 found a reported £1 billion worth of oil presently sits underneath the Queen's back garden at Windsor Castle. Who knew?

The castle is one of the monarch's state residences, and, by law, any profits would be split between the oil company and us, the people. Since a fire in 1992 destroyed large parts of the castle, it would save the taxpayer a pretty penny in repairs if the oil was drilled. And maybe they should check Balmoral for coal . . .

CANDY FLOSS

Originally called 'Fairy Floss', it was first scoffed by delighted children at the St. Louis World's Fair, today in 1898. It was a huge success, even though a single serving was half the price of admission to the entire fair. Today's candy floss is really nothing more than melted sugar and pink food colouring whirled until it extrudes itself into fine fluffy strands. It has no nutritional value whatsoever and you can practically feel your teeth dissolving with every bite. And yet, holding a stick of it cheers everyone up.

FIRST ACTRESS

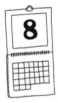

Until this day in 1660, when actress Margaret Hughes played Desdemona in *Othello*, it wasn't thought fitting for women to appear on stage. Which, given that most women of the time performed lives of housework and menial drudgery, gives you a pretty clear idea of what people thought of the acting profession.

This historic day granted women permission to perform on stage and was greeted as good news for audiences who were, I imagine, by then pretty sick and tired of watching actors fall in love with women (played by men).

SMALLPOX ERADICATED

In 1796, Dr Edward Jenner discovered how to immunise against smallpox by using a related virus, cowpox. His treatment was 95% successful, but the disease remained widespread in the developing world. In 1967 alone, it killed two million people.

The World Health Organisation had had enough and in that year mounted a globally co-ordinated assault on smallpox. Through surveillance, isolation and vaccination the international team achieved in twelve years what was previously thought unimaginable.

On this day in 1979, the disease was certified as completely eradicated.

JAPAN'S BIGGEST ROBBERY

It's 8.00a.m. this morning in 1968, and four Japanese bank employees are driving 300 million yen in bonus money to a Toshiba factory. Although it's a lot of cash, such deliveries have always gone smoothly. Suddenly, a police motorcyclist flags them down. Dynamite has apparently been planted in their car. Frightened, the employees pile out while the officer heroically crawls under the car to defuse the bomb. Unexpectedly, smoke and flames pour around their feet and the officer shouts out 'Back off, it's going to explode!' Now completely terrified, the employees leg it over the nearest wall.

Whereupon the 'cop' coolly gets into the car and drives away.

The 'flames' were from a flare.

Neither the money nor the man have ever been found.

FRANCIS DASHWOOD FINDS HELL

 Francis Dashwood would certainly have been interested to find out where he was going when he died on this day in 1781. As founder of the notorious 'Hellfire Club' – he ridiculed religion, recruited 'devils', drank heavily and enjoyed the company of many prostitutes. He was also the Chancellor of the Exchequor.

Wherever he is today, I bet he's having more fun than George Osborne.

THE MONA LISA RECOVERED, 1913

On 21 August 1911 the *Mona Lisa* – da Vinci's masterpiece – was stolen from the Louvre. It is still considered the biggest art crime in history. The police had no clues and for two years the painting remained missing.

Then today in 1913 a Florentine art dealer got a call. A man called 'Leonardo' had told the dealer he had the *Mona Lisa*. They met in a hotel room and under the man's underwear, *Lisa* was seen smiling. Police swooped in.

'Leonardo' turned out to be an ex-Louvre employee Vincenzo Peruggia. He had hidden in a broom cupboard, walked into the salon where the *Mona Lisa* hung, removed it from its frame, stuffed it up his smock and simply walked out of the museum. Vincenzo's motive was simply to return the painting to its native Italy.

Upon its return, the public went wild, and after a short tour of Italy, the world's most famous work of art was soon back smiling at the Louvre.

CLIP-ON TIE

School kids have a good reason to be happy today as the clip-on tie – which was invented by a pair of brothers in Clinton, Iowa, today in 1928 – is replacing knotted school-uniform ties. As reported by the Schoolwear Association in 2009, ten schools a week are switching to clip-on ties due to – wait for it – health and safety reasons.

LE PONT LE PLUS GRAND AU MONDE

There are just some bridges in the world that are just so cool to look at that they're worth celebrating. And the Millau Viaduct in France is at the top of the list. Formally opened today in 2004, it's the tallest bridge in the world. And it looks it. At a staggering 343m (1,125 feet!), it's taller than the Eiffel tower. It carries four lanes of autoroute 270m (886 feet) *above* the river Tarn and looks like something from the distant future. If you've never heard of it before, google it now . . .

ALFRED BIRD GETS HIS WINGS

When renowned pharmacist Alfred Bird passed away today in 1878, his respectful fellows in the Chemical Society published his obituary. They politely praised his scientific learning but couldn't bring themselves to mention Alfred's main contribution to the world – custard powder.

Bird's Custard is so ubiquitous that many British pudding fans don't realise it isn't a true custard at all – it uses cornflour instead of the traditional eggs. Alfred didn't plan on inventing a new dessert, he only whipped up a batch for his wife who was allergic to eggs. But when some guests lapped it up, he founded the famous custard brand.

BOSTON TEA PARTY

Before today's Tea Party in Boston Harbour in 1773, America was a struggling bunch of colonies taxed by a remote British Government. After today it was a rebellious young nation on the way to independence and freedom. And they have tea to thank . . .

Boston was an important trading city in the British colony of Massachusetts, but the colonists were growing increasingly tired of paying duty to a distant British king. When three shiploads of highly-taxed tea arrived at port on this day, the irate locals dumped most of it in the Harbour. This infuriated the colonial overlords, and the Revolution which was to define the USA was on . . .

LIFT OFF!

Orville and Wilbur Wright took a huge step towards their dreams today in 1903 when they flew the world's first true aeroplane.

Their inaugural flight had been short (twelve seconds), low (ten feet) and slow (seven miles per hour), but within a few years they were flying for miles and even performing figures of eight. Before he died in 1948, Orville flew in a Lockheed Constellation, noting that the wingspan of the Constellation was longer than the distance of his first flight.

BRAD PITT

Today in 1963 Brad Pitt was born. For any ladies reading, no further explanation is required.

A CHRISTMAS CAROL

Scrooge's transformation from miser to generous spirit is an uplifting tale. In fact, it's so cheery that it's one of the few books that has actually changed society. Published today in 1843, Dickens' novella helped ignite a national passion for festive generosity and more social Christmas traditions. It helped turn the season into a family-centred time of giving and merriment rather than the sombre church-based observation it had before. It even popularised the phrase 'Merry Christmas'.

INTERNATIONAL DOGSLED MAIL

When the heavy winter of 1928 made delivering the mail by normal methods pretty tricky, dogged postmaster Alden Pulsifer didn't give up, he simply created the world's first international dogsled mail service.

He took an eight-foot sled and strapped six Eskimo dogs on the front. This mutt-based mail service left Lewiston, Maine, today and arrived in Montreal on 14 January 1929. The valiant post-hounds battled through 600 miles of snowdrifts, traversed four states and visited 118 cities to deliver their Christmas post.

FIRST CROSSWORD PUBLISHED

Until this day in 1913, sadistic wordsmiths had no way of inflicting tortuous misery on poor workers who wanted a nice puzzle to liven up their tea break.

Then Arthur Wynne, an English journalist, published his 'word-cross' in the *New York World*. Diamond-shaped, it had no black squares and didn't quite grab the public's attention. But with a switcheroo of the name and a few other tweaks, the modern crossword was born and has been in pretty much every daily newspaper since.

GLOBAL ORGASM DAY

Global Orgasm, also known as GORG, is a day of action held today to coincide with the end of the winter solstice. Its founding principle is simple: all participants should have an orgasm while thinking about peace to help transmit some much needed positive energy to Earth.

Exactly how orgasming is supposed to benefit the *entire* planet is not clear, but as a line for getting someone into bed goes, it's a belter.

COELACANTH DISCOVERED

23

It's not every day that science discovers a living creature from the age of the dinosaur. Unfortunately for small children everywhere, the creature redis-covered on this day in 1938 wasn't a T-Rex but a coelacanth, an ugly-as-hell fish.

Still, it was an amazing find. Rather than hauling a haddock out of the South Atlantic, a fisherman caught an animal believed to have become extinct at the end of the Cretaceous period, sixty five million years ago.

Since then, naturalists have been pulling the things out of the sea left right and centre. Indeed, in 1999, a second species was discovered – lying on a slab in a fish market.

241

N.O.R.A.D TRACKS SANTA

When a 1955 Sears' Christmas advert printed an incorrect phone number, children started phoning the North American Aerospace Defense Command (N.O.R.A.D) hoping to speak to Santa. The kind Generals at the base didn't have the heart to disappoint the childen, so they set up a phone information service where every 24 December children could call up and ask N.O.R.A.D where Saint Nick was in the world at that time.

Of course, as word got out, these lines were flooded with thousands of excited childen. A government official soon realised that this was an inexcusable waste of US Defense manpower, and halted the phone service. Now if you want to track Santa you have to do it online at www.noradsanta.org

HARK! THE WELL-OILED ANGELS SING ...

Born on this day, a humble child who would bring hope and cheer to people the world over, and create Christmas as we know it.

That's right, today is Shane MacGowan's birthday.

BUBBLE GUM

Bubble gum is great and its existence is thanks to Walter Diemer, a twenty-three year-old bored accountant who worked for a US candy company. When Walter wasn't doing the books, he was cooking up batches of experimental gum – which is how he came up with the recipe for a gum that bubbled. He had to make the gum pink because that was the only food colouring he could find in the factory, and today in 1928, he tested it out at a small Philadelphia store – having named it 'Dubble Bubble'. The kids went wild for it.

CHARLES DARWIN SETS SAIL ON HMS BEAGLE

This five-year voyage took the young naturalist around the world to collect samples, observe landscapes and consider the ideas that he would later shape into one of science's most important theories: natural selection.

Darwin was such a diligent thinker that his methods of research extended into every aspect of his life. When considering whether or not to propose to his would-be wife, Emma, he started two new columns in his notebook, one headed *'Marry'* and the other *'Not Marry'*. Pros included 'constant companion and a friend in old age ... better than a dog anyhow', cons he noted were 'less money for books' and 'terrible loss of time'.

The old romantic.

AN INVENTOR OF REALLY USEFUL THINGS

It's wonderful when an inventor cracks one of the really big problems of life: greener cars, cheaper energy, jump jets, that sort of thing. On the other hand we should also celebrate people like Lloyd Copeman, born today in 1881, a man who dedicated his life to inventing things that simply made life a little bit more cheerful.

Like the flexible rubber ice-cube tray.

Lloyd lived the life of the eccentric inventor to the full, often locking himself in his laboratory basement for weeks on end and relying on his wife to slide meals under his door on a tray. Perhaps this contributed to his focus on contraptions that improved food and drink: he patented the first electric stove, a more efficient toaster and a device that used dry ice to cool bottles of beer.

A GEM OF A CHRISTMAS GIFT

Surprise presents can often be a little underwhelming, and you have to plaster on your best fake smile. But that wasn't the case for a New Orleans housewife called Mrs Premos who got one of the most unexpectedly brilliant presents in history on this day in 1925.

Preparing a Yuletide dinner for her family, this lucky lady set about cleaning the turkey. She put the bird on the worktop, picked up her sharpest knife and cut into the bird's neck. When she looked down she saw, sparkling amidst the gristle and gizzards, a diamond.

The gem turned out to be worth thousands of dollars. How it got there, neither Mrs Premos, the butcher, nor the turkey could say.

EDWIN HUBBLE'S OTHER GALAXIES

Since there's nothing bigger than the Universe, technically, this was the biggest discovery of all time. Today in 1924, astronomer Edwin Hubble pointed out that in galactic terms, we aren't alone, bending even the best minds and making the cosmos a more fantastical place than we had ever imagined.

Before Hubble's discoveries, astronomers thought that the Universe consisted entirely of the Milky Way Galaxy. But, using the World's largest telescope, Hubble deduced that several nebulae were far too distant to be part of the Milky Way, and our galaxy was actually just one in a seemingly never-ending eternity of galaxies.

Hubble also later showed that the Universe is expanding, which helped develop the Big Bang Theory.

NEW YEAR'S EVE

New Year's Eve is a corker of a day for being cheery. It's a time of transition, fresh beginnings, family reunions, celebrations and colossally epic boozing.

Appropriately enough, given the spectacular light shows and fireworks that light up the skies at midnight tonight, today was also the day in 1897 that Thomas Edison gave the world light. Well, the lightbulb.

ACKNOWLEDGEMENTS

To my son, Harry, who makes me cheerful every day.

Thanks to Rachel for support, love and putting up
with the fact-spouting.
To my father, Mark, for encouraging me to look things up.
To Margaret and Nigel Bullen and Gill Levy for
supreme babysitting.
To Malcolm Croft, for making the fun actually happen.